DEEP AS THE OCEAN

DEEP AS THE OCEAN

From local girl to international star is a big step for any young woman, and Linda's brilliance as a swimmer, combined with her beauty and charm, make her a coveted prize for both men in her life. Andy Blane, unscrupulous and sophisticated, takes an interest in her career but when she meets the fabulous film promoter Max, life takes a romantic turn. Andy for reasons of his own, conceals Max's true identity from Linda, but their mutual attraction is proof against his scheming.

Deep As The Ocean

by

Cora Mayne

Dales Large Print Books
Long Preston, North Yorkshire,
BD23 4ND, England.

British Library Cataloguing in Publication Data.

Mayne, Cora
    Deep as the ocean.

    A catalogue record of this book is
    available from the British Library

    ISBN   978-1-84262-867-6 pbk

First published in Great Britain in 1966
by John Gresham Limited

Published in Large Print 2012 by arrangement with
S. Walker Literary Agency

Dales Large Print is an imprint of Library Magna Books Ltd.

Printed and bound in Great Britain by
T.J. (International) Ltd., Cornwall, PL28 8RW

Chapter 1

'Aunt Mary, have a heart!' Linda Ross laughed, in mock dismay, as she pegged her swimming things on the line in the little paved back garden, and surveyed the scene through the open window of her aunt's kitchen. 'I can't eat all that marvellous array of things if I'm going in for the swimming contest on Saturday! It's more than I dare do!'

'Oh, what a shame!' her aunt sighed, pushing back a lock of dark hair from her hot forehead. 'I've set such a store on this holiday of yours, and I did so want to do all my best cooking for you! You don't get this sort of thing at home, I'll warrant!'

Linda chuckled as she walked round to the open door and came into the kitchen. 'You're right there! With our size family, Mum just about has enough on her hands with plain cooking, let alone all this fancy stuff. Ah, you're a darling, but don't tempt me. Not until after this weekend, anyway!'

Mrs Goodge looked fondly at her favourite

niece. 'You are a one, Linda! You've fair set your heart on winning those old races at the baths, haven't you? All the years I've lived in Shenstone Bay, and watched them do away with the old baths and build that fine new Open-Air bath, I never thought that one day my own niece would enter the Carnival Competition there! I hope you win, duck, that I do!'

'Well, don't set your hopes too high, that's all!' Linda warned. 'Lots of the other competitors were there today, and too many of them can do as well as I can. When it comes to the day, I shall find I'm not so good after all.'

'Never mind, love; to go in for the thing when you want it as badly as all that, is half the battle, I always say. Funny, you being so keen on swimming. Oh, the rest of the family is good at it, I'll grant, but the others are keen on everything in the way of sport, whereas with you it's always been the water and nothing else. Even since your Uncle Zacchary put you in the water as a kiddie and you kicked out and kept yourself afloat! You won't remember that. You were only three.'

'No, I don't remember it, but I've heard about it till I could tell the story by heart!'

Linda retorted.

'Well, who can blame me for being so proud? My own brother, too. You know, he's a remarkable man, though I say it as shouldn't. We never thought he'd do anything active again after he fell off that scaffolding and got lame. We thought it'd break his heart, being such a keen swimmer. You could have knocked me down with a feather, when I heard he'd got himself a job as attendant at the baths in Crackington. Does he ever speak about his swimming days, Linda, love?'

'Sometimes. Not often,' Linda admitted thoughtfully. 'I think the best thing that happened to him was when we moved over to Crackington and he came to live with us. He dotes on the boys. The most awful thing that could happen to him would be if one of us said we hated water,' she finished, laughing. 'Where's my other swimsuit?'

'Linda! You're never going back to the baths again today? You'll tire yourself out!'

'I just want to get my things ready for this evening. I'm going to have a nice quiet swim in the sea. Not practice. Just to enjoy myself,' Linda said. 'I've got to get as much out of this holiday as I can – and here's the first week half gone already!'

'One thing, the weather's just about all

you could wish for,' her aunt remarked, pouring a second cup of tea for Linda and amply sugaring it. 'It's the first bit of really hot weather we've had this season. I do hope it keeps like this for the Carnival. It's going to be on television this year! I just wish you could have been on one of the floats, instead of hiding that pretty hair of yours under that plain old swimcap of yours!' her aunt sighed.

'It's not an old cap, and it's got to be a plain one,' Linda scolded, pushing the tea away untouched. 'Besides, I'd rather swim, Aunt Mary!'

'Yes, I know you would, dear! You know, you're the spitting image of me as a girl. Look at this photo I got out the other day.'

Linda looked over her aunt's shoulder, slipping a friendly arm round her as the older woman got out of the dresser drawer a picture of a young woman in the fashion of the twenties. But as she pointed out, the main details of both that face and her niece's were strikingly similar.

'The same dark hair, you see – all springy and wavy – couldn't do a thing with it! The same with you, duck – ah, I know how much you want one of those smooth upsweeps all swathed round the head, that you young girls are so fond of nowadays, but bless you, it wouldn't do you any good if you had that sort of hair. Not in the water, I mean! You'd never get a swimcap to fit, and you'd get so fed-up having all that straight hair to get dry and fixed again!'

'Better than this short unruly mop!' Linda protested.

'Go on! The chaps like naturally curly hair! Funny, even your eyes are like mine – well, mine *were* that bright blue years ago. (They're a bit faded now.) And that saucy little turn-up nose, too! Even the determined chin. My poor husband used to say he wanted his head searching for marrying a girl with a chin like that. Mulish, he called me. Well, determination would be a better word. And you've got it, too, duck, and don't you take any notice if anyone says it's a bad thing. It's not. Any girl as ambitious as you are, needs determination in this life!'

It was true, Linda reflected, as she dried her hair later in front of the little dressing-table in her aunt's spare bedroom, and tried to get the comb through the thick tight waves and curly ends. Linda's brothers were always teasing her for being so determined. But supposing men didn't really like a girl to be so determined?

Linda, at seventeen, had never had a boy friend. All her thoughts and energy had been directed towards swimming while her girl friends liked dancing and shows. Linda – who didn't use make-up and relied on the glowing health in her face – often felt rather left out.

She shrugged and thought of other things. The wild end of the bay, beyond the town, where the Giant's Teeth lay. These – a gaunt pile of rocks, with a sheltered pool in the middle, were a good walk away from the last of the shops and amusement places, and usually deserted. Linda decided to go there that evening for a bathe.

Shenstone Bay was a complete novelty to her. Her family had left here when she had been quite little, and Crackington where they now lived, was an industrial town in the Midlands, far away from this lovely line of coast. She wished they could have stayed here, but her father had been alive then, and the offer of a good job in a factory had tempted him to move his family. Now they were settled there, the boys all had jobs there; Linda and her mother, too. They couldn't afford to move back to the coast.

It was a perfect evening for swimming. The tide had receded, leaving the water among the Giant's Teeth clean and clear, reflecting the pinkish blue colour of the evening sky, as the sun was beginning to set.

Linda had the place to herself as she had hoped. She shed her raincoat and pulled on her green swim cap. Her new swimsuit, green and blue patterned, was a pleasant change after the regulation navy one she had been wearing for serious swimming in the baths during the day, and it was with a sense of complete relaxation that she dived cleanly into the deep pool.

The water was pleasantly cool after the heat of the day. Linda surfaced and lay floating and, as she did so, she became aware of a young man standing up on the flat top of one of the larger rocks.

She trod water, shading her eyes against the settling sun, and looked up at him. He was young, not too tall, but his slight build made him appear tall. He was immaculately dressed – a little too smart for Linda's taste – but his lean, clean-shaven face and friendly creased-up smile made up for this.

He waved cheerily at her. 'Don't mind me! I've just discovered this spot! Rather unexpected, isn't it, in a town like Shenstone Bay?'

Linda nodded, uncertain what to do. Her

best friend, who had a great deal of poise, would have known just how to turn on the charm and bring that young man down from his lofty perch, and would have had a date made in no time at all.

Linda was furious with herself for being so tongue-tied. At seventeen, she was really only comfortable with boys of her own age who swam. The swimming enthusiasts were so different from this sophisticated type of young man.

'Do you live here, or are you just staying?' he persevered, but he made no attempt to come down nearer to her. Probably afraid of damaging those knife-pressed pale fawn trousers, or getting green stains on his jacket from the slime on the rocks.

'Staying with my aunt, who lives here!' she admitted. And because of the awkward pause which followed that, Linda resumed her swimming and took no more notice of him.

He stood watching her. It was a long time since he had seen a girl playing about in water with the abandon of a fish, especially as she had been doing it before she realised she had an audience. He was convinced that she was as unconscious of her grace and strength in the water, as she was of breath-

14

ing. Good-looking, too, he decided, but as simple and unspoiled as a schoolgirl.

Perhaps she was just a schoolgirl, he reasoned, frowning. Although she had a good figure, her diffidence and complete lack of make-up made it difficult to decide her age. Regretfully he decided that such absence of sophistication could only mean that she was much younger than he had at first thought.

Linda dived underneath. His standing there staring down at her made her edgy. She wished he would go. She had wanted this marvellous place all to herself.

'Why don't you go and look at the new Open-Air pool?' she called, surfacing and shaking her head like a puppy. 'It's super!'

Her frown endorsed his recent opinion. No, she was no good for his purposes, he shrugged. 'Perhaps I will!' he called, smiling broadly. 'Well, goodbye! Enjoy your swim, and don't stay in too long! It'll get chilly after sundown!'

Linda flushed with anger and chagrin. Who did he think he was, giving her advice as if she were a kid?

She watched him pick his way carefully to the top, but he didn't look back as he vanished behind the tall rocks.

He had spoiled her swim, so she came out,

tore off her cap and rubbed the offending hair, which now stood on end like a doll's. That sort of encounter merely pressed home the constant advice of her best friend, who was always scolding Linda for spending all her spare time and money on swimming. 'You're not with it!' Elaine would always say. 'You want to get a facial, trim those thick brows, and do something to that hair! And how about getting a line of small talk? You'll never get a boy at this rate!'

I don't want a boy, I just want to get to the top, swimming! Linda would say to herself. I don't quite know what sort of top I want to reach, but I want to get there just the same!

She forgot about the young man in the next few days. Her whole thoughts were bent on the Swimming Gala on the Saturday.

'It's a pity you didn't manage to get a bit of training first, love,' her aunt commented, as they sat at breakfast on the morning of the Gala. 'Your Uncle Zacchary ought to have been on holiday at the same time – he'd have given you a few tips.'

'But that's the whole point, Aunt Mary!' Linda protested. 'You're not eligible if you've had any training! Not for this Gala, anyway. It's strictly for amateurs – people

16

who are on holiday. I know! I've read the rules till I know them by heart, but aren't I glad I happened to get my holiday at the same time as the Gala! If that girl in my office hadn't swapped dates, I might have been back home by now!'

'We might not have had the Gala anyway, if Peacock Cosmetics hadn't sponsored it, our local Council is so unimaginative!' her aunt said. 'Mind you, not many folk like the idea. Peacock Cosmetics is a new firm, not local people at all. Still, the advertisements ought to do the town some good. Wouldn't it be fine if you got the First Prize, love? Two hundred and fifty pounds, isn't it?'

'I shan't, don't worry! But I'd settle for the Second Prize any day,' Linda laughed. In her heart, that was her secret target, that fifty pounds second prize. If she could only pull that off, she could get the handsome washing machine she knew her mother yearned for, in the showrooms in the Crackington High Street!

'What events did you enter for then, love?' her aunt asked, laughing at her niece's modesty.

'Three events – the things I'm best at. Women's medley (I shall do breast stroke), free style diving and back crawl.'

'Won't all that be too much for you?'

'I don't think so. I don't get tired if I'm doing the strokes I like.'

'Then how do they decide who's won that money prize – that's what I can't make out,' Mrs Goodge protested.

'The one who's won the most events gets the First Prize, but style also counts,' Linda explained.

That Saturday was going to be scorching hot, hotter than the rest of the week had been, Linda thought happily, as at last the time came to go to the Open-Air Swimming Baths.

Already the spectators were gathering. It was a beautiful swimming bath, gleaming with white paint and chromium, excellent diving apparatus and seating accommodation. The polished metal and the brilliant colours in the flags and bunting hurt the eyes in the glare of the sunlight on the blue lined pool.

Mrs Goodge had spent most of the morning with the crowds lining the pavements watching the Carnival procession, but Linda had taken it easily. Even the television cameras in the town couldn't tempt her to put out as much energy as usual. She just had to keep fresh for the afternoon!

When at last the time came to go to the baths, she felt her high hopes evaporating. She felt depressed about her chances. The other competitors all seemed so confident. She was puzzled, too, by the sight of the young man who had been watching her from the rocks the other night; he stood talking now to one of the men with the television cameras, and wandered away without having appeared to have noticed her.

When they were set on their marks for the Women's Medley, however, Linda's mind cleared, and her depression ebbed away. This was her favourite event, which she felt she would really enjoy.

Three of the competitors weren't so polished as she had anticipated, but the other two were very good. Linda had watched them all in earlier events. The one on her left was the one to watch; the girl's breast-stroke was superb.

It was a gruelling race. Linda was neck and neck with the second girl at the first turn; she fell a little behind at the second turn, but put out all she had for the third length and tied with the second girl.

With her diving she fared better. She loved diving, and although she didn't realise it, her performance was a delight to watch. She got a lot of applause.

The testing time for her was the back crawl race. She had watched sporting events on television and taken note of her uncle's shrewd comments on the competitors, and she had learned one important thing; that in a three-length race the great thing is to save one's best effort for the last length.

To this end she had been practising in the unfamiliar surroundings of the new Open-Air Bath all that week, and getting used to little personal landmarks, checking them by the big clock at each end of the baths.

It was a rough-and-ready kind of self-training, but that – added to her own superb natural style and speed – carried her through today. In the first length she touched the end of the baths at the same time as three of the other five competitors; in the second length she was holding her own with the second fastest girl, but the first girl was some way ahead. Then came the last length, and to Linda's amazement, the leading competitor was noticeably tiring. Linda slowly and painfully reduced the intervening space between them minute by agonising minute, but still the other girl held on to the lead.

Linda forgot that she had set her target for coming second. It was imperative now, that she should win. The encouraging shouts and shrieks of excitement of the spectators were to Linda no more than a subdued roar. All she was aware of was the girl in the next lane but one. They might have been alone in the baths, for all that Linda knew or cared.

They kept neck and neck until almost the end. Then, in the last few yards, Linda found strength for a last stupendous effort, and touched down at what she thought was the same split second as her rival.

The crowd went wild. 'You've won! You've won!' someone shouted near at hand. 'Stay in the water.'

Linda thought that meant her rival had won, but it was her hand someone was stooping down to grasp and wring. The other girl came through the ropes and put an exhausted hand on her shoulder. Linda herself had never been so tired in her life. She still thought that it was the other girl's race, until she said, with rueful laughter. 'That was great! You had me licked!'

'I thought it was you who had won!' Linda said, but she was really too tired to care now.

They were told to get out of the water, and someone folded a towelling gown round Linda's shoulders. She was shivering, although the sun was so hot.

Someone was shouting through the mega-phone, and the crowd was applauding again, but all Linda wanted to do was to sit down somewhere quietly and get her breath back. She had put far more effort into that last race than she had realised.

There were three more events, and then the Gala was over. The exciting part came now. Who would get the prizes?

There was a lot of talk going on between the sponsors and the judges. A fussy little man rushed up and down, looking at his notes and comparing them with those of other people.

Then someone came and told Linda to go to the end where the television cameras were, and the platform where the competitors would receive the prizes. Amid applause and shouting, Linda heard with complete bewil-derment the announcement: 'The First Prize of two hundred and fifty pounds generously presented by the manufacturers of Peacock Cosmetics goes to the little girl who charmed us all by her beautiful style and good looks as well as her swimming technique: *Linda Ross!*'

Max Welman stretched his legs. He was bored, horribly bored. He wished he had stayed at his usual hotel in Shenstone Bay, instead of allowing himself, against his better judgment, to be persuaded to stay with the Chadwicks at their luxury seaside house further down the coast.

He was a handsome young man, tall, with dark hair just beginning to be touched with silver at the temples. He had the easy and confident manner of a man who has already acquired great wealth through astuteness in business. He had wide interests which took him to many places, where he met far too many pretty girls who were convinced that if only he would back them financially, they would be destined for stardom. And because he valued Joe Chadwick's friendship, he had to be nice to Joe's daughter Caroline, although she bored him excessively. Joe Chadwick had helped Max with sound advice when he had been young and a beginner at the game.

So Max absently played with Caroline Chadwick's heavy corn-gold hair while he stared at the television screen in her father's ornate sun lounge, and consoled himself with the thought that he would be going back to London tomorrow.

The television programme was one of a mixed seaside Carnival event. Starting with Silvercove and going on to Rockhurst where there was a regatta as well, the cameras suddenly switched back to Shenstone Bay, to the new Open-Air Swimming Pool, at the precise moment when Linda was doing a difficult but competent swallow dive.

Caroline felt Max stiffen and he dropped his hand from her head and sat up. 'That was nice – very nice,' he murmured, half to himself.

'Lean back, darling, and take it easy,' Caroline murmured. 'It's only a local amateur show. Nothing to get excited about. I don't know why we've got it turned on.'

'Sh-h!' he said. 'I want to see this.'

She knew she had lost his attention so she got up and crossed the room to turn off the set.

'Don't turn it off, please, Caroline!' he said sharply as he leaned forward in his chair.

It was a new experience for Caroline to be alone with Max and to feel his attention riveted to some unknown girl on the television screen.

'Max!' she said sharply. 'You shouted at me!'

'Caro, Caro, don't you see? That girl's *got* something! Who the deuce is she? Don't they put competitors' names anywhere?'

'Of course not, Max darling. They're just

holiday makers! The sort of people who will never be heard of again!'

He turned sharply and looked at her, as if he had never seen her before.

'Don't you believe it, my dear Caro!' he said, with such certainty that Caroline suddenly felt afraid.

With increasing uneasiness, she watched his face as he sat riveted to the screen. When Max let his attention be caught like this, one could do nothing with him.

He patiently viewed through the rest of the events, and with evident pleasure watched Linda Ross's smooth rapid cleaving through the water in an easy winning of the last race, and when Linda was hailed as the winner of the cheque for two hundred and fifty pounds, and the television cameras trained on her and brought her face into close-up, Caroline heard Max take a sharp breath.

She stared at Linda's face on the screen, wanting badly to discover what the girl had, to take Max's fancy like this. All Caroline saw was a very young – touchingly young – countenance, dazed with this sudden slice of good fortune; a young girl with ordinary prettiness over-ridden by such eagerness that it hurt to watch her.

Max, on the other hand, saw a superb

young figure and a face deeply etched with character, from the smooth high forehead to the formidable little chin. He liked what he saw, particularly the sudden sweet wide smile as Linda acknowledged the shouts and cheers of the watching people.

'Totally unaffected by all this,' Max murmured, half to himself. 'A lovely child. And what swimming! What diving!'

The interviewer at the Shenstone Baths was enjoying himself, too. 'You look surprised, Linda. Didn't you think you'd won?'

Max waited breathlessly to hear her answer. The voice was so important.

'No, I couldn't believe it!' Linda admitted, and Max Welman – listening and watching avidly – gave an entranced sigh.

'What will you do with the money?' Linda was asked.

'I don't know!' she said. 'I'd gone all out for the Second Prize of fifty pounds – that was what I needed.'

'Any use asking why?' the interviewer smiled. 'Or is it a secret?' He, too, had taken an instant liking to Linda.

'Yes, it is actually,' she said, engagingly. 'It's something for my mother, but I can't say what, in case she's looking in!'

'Does she know about today?'

'No!' Linda gasped, laughing. 'I didn't write home and tell her, in case I did badly.'

'You did very well!' the interviewer assured her.

'She did indeed!' Max Welman agreed, as Linda was faded off the screen.

And so Caroline was hardly surprised when, the Carnival televising over, so far as Shenstone Bay was concerned, Max jumped up.

'Darling, I've got to go!' he announced, his face alive, as eager as the face of that young swimmer at the Open-Air Baths. 'I must find Tim Ripley at once. Forgive me – see you later!'

He didn't wait to hear what Caroline had to say about that. Caroline knew better than to call him back, too.

She knew he was going to take that girl up. She had seen him like this before. Max, among other things, was a star-maker when the mood took him.

She sat coldly thinking it over. Not now, but later, she would get to work on him, to wean him away – not only from that young swimmer and her silly un-made-up face, Caroline told herself fiercely, but away from all this promoting of his, that took so much of his attention away from herself.

Chapter 2

The excitement and the noise swept Linda along on a tide. Aunt Mary was almost in tears of happiness. Friends and neighbours with her were dancing for joy. Nothing like this had happened to them before.

Someone urged Linda along to the dressing-rooms for a shower and quick rub down. Interviewers were wanting a word with her. Personnel of the baths, including some bigwigs from the local Council. Only one of them had any interest for Linda, and that was the young man who had watched her on the rocks that evening.

He wasn't looking at her now as if she were a mere schoolgirl. He was looking at her with admiration and a new interest that was flattering, and also filled her with sudden embarrassment, and set her heart beating in a queer sort of way.

She was glad so many people were all talking at once, urging her away to get rubbed down and dressed.

She went with them, borne along by the

excitement, and a queer feeling rather like an oncoming depression that was, her Uncle Zacchary could have told her, the aftermath of the effort she had put out to win, and the ultimate success.

When she was dressed and ready, she just wanted to escape from the crowds, go home to Aunt Mary's to think it all over, discuss it with her aunt in the quiet comfortable kitchen and to have a glorious hot cup of tea.

She wondered what her family were thinking, if they had been able to see the television. She found herself wondering what her father would have said, had he been alive. She could hardly remember him, it was so long ago. Her Uncle Zacchary had almost come to take his place, at least where such things as advice or approval were concerned. Would Uncle Zacchary approve of today's events? She wasn't really sure.

She couldn't reach her Aunt Mary where she was standing on the steps. She waved, and her aunt spotted her, and signalled that she would go home and start the meal.

Linda nodded and, caught in a press of laughing and chattering people who seemed to be wedged at a standstill, she doubled back, and left by climbing over a rail and dropping down on to the beach.

Someone jumped down after her, helping her up as she struggled to recover herself. It had been a deeper drop than she had at first realised and she had gone over on to her hands and knees.

'You are a mad little devil!' a laughing voice said, and she looked up to find the young man again; the one who had been watching her in the pool. 'I thought you were only a school-kid until I saw you entered in the higher age groups today! Why do you behave like a tomboy?'

She flushed and shrugged. 'It's my way, that's all!'

'You didn't like it when I watched you in the pool, the other evening, either, did you? I'm sorry if I disturbed your privacy, but frankly, I was enchanted with your perform-ance in the water. You really are very good indeed, you know!'

'It's all right. You startled me, that's all,' Linda said, and hated herself for her blunt speech. She couldn't help it. He at once interested her but at the same time put her back up, and her resentment and indigna-tion won.

'You don't look in a very forgiving mood, but maybe you could do with a cup of tea. I know I could! Let's go and find one, shall we – away from the crowds? Or are you expecting someone?'

He was so smooth and charming, he made her feel thoroughly awkward and gauche. Without waiting for her answer, he took her left hand and turned it over. 'No engagement ring, I see. So may I escort you?'

'I was actually on my way back to my aunt's for tea,' Linda confessed. 'But I couldn't get through the crowds.'

'Is your aunt waiting for you?'

'No. She went off home to start a meal.'

'Then let's nip over to the Imperial for a nice private cup of tea and a chat. They have a rather nice shady balcony with jolly tables set out.'

The Imperial was a massive white stone edifice behind incredibly well-kept lawns, beyond the Open-Air Baths. The quiet end of the town, beyond the reach of the shore where the pleasure boats and the ice-cream booths were. Their private strip of beach was railed off, and there were striped umbrellas, beneath which the residents lay sun-bathing on air mattresses all day. The hotel had a uniformed porter at the revolving door too.

Linda had never been there before, and she looked down in dismay at her dress;

freshly starched and laundered for this morning, but after being trampled on the damp floor of the changing room, a sad and sorry sight now.

'Never mind that,' he said, reading her thoughts. 'Just concentrate on your success today. That should make you feel on top of the world, especially when you hear what I want to talk to you about! By the way, let me introduce myself. My name is Blane – Andy Blane. I'm the sort of chap who can spot a winner any day. And according to the announcement at the Baths, your name is Linda Ross.'

Before the onslaught of his charm and persuasion, and also because she was very tired indeed, Linda made no further attempt at argument, but let Andy Blane escort her to the hotel.

The porter, whom Andy apparently knew, appeared quite kindly, especially when Andy said, 'This is Miss Ross, the winner this afternoon at the Baths – in person!'

'Very nice performance if I may say so, miss,' the porter said. 'We all watched you on the telly.'

The balcony was gloriously cool and shady, with a view of the Bay – really blue today under the blinding glare of a cloudless sky –

and there was hardly a sail to be seen anywhere. Only the little speedboats leaving a bigger white trail in their wake than themselves. The air was filled with the drone of the Air-Sea Rescue helicopter, and the screech of seagulls. And there was a full week's holiday left.

Linda sat back with a sigh of pure pleasure. The tea was brought by an elderly waiter, and Andy poured from the big silver tea-pot. Wafer-thin cucumber sandwiches and small cream puffs were a welcome sight, and he tactfully waited till Linda had had her tea, before he went on talking.

Then he began to talk. Not exactly fast talking, but swift assured conversation that swept away the early doubts that Linda had had about him.

'My father is Thomas Blane. I daresay you've heard about him. No? Well, let me assure you that he's a very big name in the world of show business. He's a hard man to please, but I think he'll be very glad to hear about you, Linda. The first time I saw you swimming, I thought to myself, the miracle's happened!'

'Miracle?' she echoed, blankly.

'If that sounds rather overdone, let me assure you that it isn't really. You can find wonderful swimmers, who have no other asset. You can find extremely good-looking girls, with nothing else but their looks. Some girls have a nice figure, some are blessed with a marvellous voice. Some have got personality but none of the other things. But in you – and I can't really believe it myself yet! – we appear to have got the lot! I'm sure there's a snag somewhere, but I'm keeping my fingers crossed, hoping against hope that there isn't!'

'I think you're talking an awful lot of nonsense,' Linda said quietly, with heightened colour. She wasn't used to such praise and wasn't sure that she liked or trusted it.

'If I sound like that, then I've failed in my own particular job,' he said earnestly, 'but somehow I don't think I have. I think it's just your terrific modesty.'

She shook her head. 'Look, Mr Blane–'

'Oh, call me Andy, do!'

'I can't. I don't know you well enough, and to be frank, I don't see much point in knowing you. I hope that doesn't sound ill-mannered, but it's a fact. Look at me – I've just managed to win a competition. I can't think how, but I have, and I'm pretty sure it's just a slice of luck! Well, that's it! The lot!'

'What d'you mean, *that's it?*' he asked, amused.

'That's just what I do mean, Mr Blane. I've had no training. I just swim because I love it. I started at three and I just happened to take to it. But my holiday will be over in a week's time, and I shall be going back to my job in my home town. I shan't come here again until next year (if I'm lucky!) to stay with my aunt again. There's nothing in all that to get you so excited.'

'You mean you haven't been trained for the stage or dancing or elocution or any swimming at all?'

'No. My family couldn't afford it, even if I'd wanted it.'

'You astonish me! You shock me, too, Linda, to think a girl with all the assets you have, should resign yourself to a job in some town – what *is* your job by the way?'

'I serve in a shoe shop,' she said shortly.

'Then that's all right,' he said coolly. 'What I mean is, there'll be no nonsense about a career to give up, if and when my father wants to start in on boosting you to the top!'

'But how can your father, who you say is in show business, have any use for a girl who's won a swimming competition?'

'My dear Linda, there are limitless possibilities for someone like you! Water shows, demonstrations at country clubs, summer entertainment all round the coast – the circus and pantomime – Linda, don't you *want* to earn big money, see your name in lights?'

He patted her hand as she continued to stare at him. 'You really are a poppet – you just can't take it in that you're on the brink of big things, can you? Now, if you've finished your tea, I'll run you home. I expect you like plenty of time to get changed – most girls do!'

'Changed for what? I'm not going anywhere.'

'Of course you are! You're coming dancing tonight! With me!' He smiled down into her outraged face. 'You have to celebrate, you know! Everyone expects it! I thought we might come back here. There's a good dance band and the chances are that an enterprising cameraman might be around, and he'll want to get a shot of my partner. They usually do.'

There was an astonished pause. 'You think you've got me where you want me, don't you? Is this your usual line with girls who win competitions? If so, don't waste your time with me. I don't care for that sort of thing.'

'I didn't think you would, somehow,' he

said, pulling a face. 'Any use me saying I'm lonely and that you were the only girl I felt I wanted to be with? No? That won't work either! Oh, well, I'd better come clean, then.'

He drew a deep breath. 'Right, then here it is! My father isn't anyone important in show business. (I took a chance with that, hoping you wouldn't know any better!) I haven't got a father, to be honest. But I'm trying to find someone to push, and incidentally get myself somewhere too. When I saw you in the Baths, I decided you were a sure winner, and if I could get in first, tell you the tale, and make a star of you, there'd be big money in it for me too!'

'Is that the truth?' she asked, after a shocked silence.

'That's it! Not very pretty, is it?'

'What do you do for a living, Andy?'

'I work in a variety agent's office,' he admitted.

Suddenly she smiled, and held out her hand. 'Then shake on it! What are we waiting for? Push me, right to the top!'

His astonishment was ludicrous. 'You kidding?'

'No! Not now – but why on earth didn't you tell me the truth at first? I'd rather be starting out with another beginner, than feel

I was at the mercy of a big shot who was just using me! Besides, I'm blunt – I like other people to be, as well.'

'Well, atta girl!' he said, shaking her hand, then on second thoughts giving her a swift hug. 'You're a poppet. Let's go places!'

Andy's idea of the truth wasn't entirely Linda's. She found out that the good time he was laying on for her was really being laid on by the makers of Peacock Cosmetics, for all the Carnival winners. Still, he made a good companion, and they had a wonderful week, not all spent in the public eye, or indeed with the other competition winners. Sometimes they went swimming together, at dawn, in Linda's private pool by the Giant's Teeth. Sometimes they hired a small motorboat and went fishing. Andy was good fun by any standards.

Mrs Goodge liked him, too. 'What I say, love, is to have a good time while you can! You never know what lies around the corner!'

'What d'you mean by that, Aunt Mary?'

'Don't sound so scared, love,' her aunt hastily assured her. 'I was only talking in a general way. You've worked very hard and not had much fun in your young life. Well, now you've met a nice lad like Andy Blane, and you're on top of the world! Enjoy it, while it lasts! That's all! Well, if you must know, I've always had a queer feeling about good times just when you're on top, something seems to come along and slap you down. Well, it always did with me, but with you it might be different. I only hope so!'

Linda laughed at her aunt's fears, until the day before she was due to go home. A telegram came for her.

'Lawks, how those things do upset me!' her aunt exclaimed, one hand dramatically on her chest. 'What does it say, love?'

'You can read it. It's from Uncle Zacchary. Mother's been taken ill. He doesn't say what's wrong with her but he seems to think that I might not be coming back home because of all the publicity. But I was going home, just the same!'

'Don't be so upset, Linda, duck! I'm sure our Zacchary would have said in the telegram if it was real urgent. And you're going home tomorrow, anyway!'

'No! No, I can't wait for tomorrow, Aunt Mary! I must go tonight. There's a train – I'll fling my things in a bag. I can just catch it. Oh, Aunt Mary, there's Andy! Oh, you see him and explain. I'll give you the number of his room at the hotel. He'll want to persuade me to stay till tomorrow – he had

39

several things laid on for the last day. I can't see him – you see him, will you?'

After a lot of persuading, Mrs Goodge allowed that it might be for the best, and after she had seen Linda off on the evening train, she went back to see Andy Blane at his modest hotel at the back of the town.

Linda made the journey home with mixed feelings. She had never known her mother to be ill, never known any of her family to have the need to send a telegram. Nothing seemed to have happened of any importance since the death of her father.

Her uncle was due to be leaving the Baths, so she walked that way home from the station, to speak to him first about her mother. When he came out of the Baths, she saw he looked grave.

He was a tall man, with rugged pleasantly ugly features, thinning dark hair and a pronounced limp. His face lit a little as he caught sight of Linda.

'Oh, there you are, girl! I was hoping you'd come back tonight. We've had a fine old time, I can tell you! But how are you, then?'

'I'm fine, just fine! But what about Mum?'

'I think she'll be all right, lass, but she's got to have quiet to get over it.'

'Get over *what?*'

'The shock of it all. It took us all of a heap!'

'I don't know what you're talking about, Uncle!'

'Well, it's this swimming business, Linda. We didn't know about it–'

'But I didn't want any of you to know, in case I didn't make the grade!' Linda protested. 'Is that what upset Mum?'

'Well, no, not the swimming so much. We were all rare glad about that part of it, especially the boys. Proud as Punch they were. No, it was what followed after it. All the publicity. You on telly. Then that chap who came. That was what really started your Mum getting ill. Just collapsed, she did. Never seen her like it before. We had to have the doctor, and he said she'd just got to have rest and not be worried any more.'

'Uncle, *what* man? You don't mean Andy Blane! You can't – he's been with me practically all the time since last Saturday!'

'Andy Blane? Who's he?' her Uncle asked sharply.

'He's a young man I met – a sort of promoter I suppose you'd call him. He's going to groom me, see I get to the top. You know the sort of thing!'

'Is he!' her uncle retorted. 'Then that's

41

another one! I knew this would happen, as soon as you were televised. It's always the same. Why can't they let a young girl alone?'

'But this man – the one who upset Mum!' Linda insisted.

'Oh, yes. Well, it was on the Monday, and he came unexpected. Dapper chap, late thirties, I suppose. Said his name was Ripley – Tim Ripley, and that he was representing some big shot called Max Welman. Ever heard of him, Linda? No, neither have I. Well, he was a smooth talker all right.'

'But what did he want, and why come home? Why not see me?' Linda expostulated.

'Ah, well, they didn't seem to know where to find you in Shenstone Bay. Seems you only gave your home address when you filled up the entry form for the Competition. That's how they got it. Well, this chap Ripley sings your praises, how they saw you on television, and his boss was on the look-out for actors in a water film. Usually they have someone who can swim, doubling for the star, but you took the big shot's fancy and he wanted to groom you for the acting part too!'

'Me! On the films!' Linda gasped.

'Yes, well, don't get excited, lass. We didn't

think much to it, your Mum and me, and we were going to talk it over and turn it down, when after he'd gone, a girl comes. What was her name? Oh, yes, Chadwick. Caroline Chadwick. Well, what she had to say, not only put us right against the idea, but upset your mother into the bargain!'

'What on earth did she say, then?'

'Well, it appears she won something similar to you, and they took her up, and she was never more sorry, she said. Oh, the things she told us, you wouldn't credit. Well, it wasn't any news to me – I've heard tales like that before. Taking the girls up, treating 'em badly, and leaving 'em – most of them are real glad to get back to their old lives. But your Mum was so upset, she just pleaded with me to talk you out of wanting to do anything that anyone might suggest to you.'

'Gosh, I had no idea! I'm sorry Mum's upset, Uncle, but you might have both asked me how I felt about it first. I mean, there wasn't any need to worry. I wouldn't have done anything in a hurry. Besides, there's Andy Blane.'

'And what does he think he's going to do with you by way of a future?' her uncle asked bluntly.

43

'There are all sorts of things a swimmer with good looks can do in the entertainment world, he says,' Linda began but her uncle cut her short.

'There you are again! The entertainment world! It won't do, lass! Now listen, before you say anything, I've got a proposition to make, and I think it might appeal to you. I'm glad I had this chance of talking to you, before you see your Mother. Now look – swimming's been my life. Right?'

'Right,' she agreed, her disappointment only too clear.

'Well, then, how would it be if I trained you for good honest competitive swimming? I think I could! And I think from what I've seen and heard, that you'd be good enough. But you'd have to work hard, now! And no nonsense about good times and boy friends and gadding about. Just hard work.'

'Competitive swimming?' Linda frowned. It sounded rather technical, and she wasn't sure about it at all.

'I would have mentioned it before, but I never thought you'd sustain a public race, my girl. You always swim and fool about in the water just to please yourself, and I just didn't think you'd got it in you. Well, now you've proved you can compete with the best, I'll take you on. You set your sights on a particular line, then you train for it. You work your way up, race by race, championship by championship. And if you've got it in you, before you're too old, there's the Olympics at the top. Now, does that attract you?'

'Olympics?' Linda breathed, looking up at him with shining eyes. Andy Blane's rather airy promises began to melt away, before her Uncle's concrete suggestions. 'Oh, yes, that does sound *something!*' she said, nodding her head. 'Yes, now you're *talking*, Uncle!'

Chapter 3

Linda's mother was sitting up in bed. Linda couldn't remember seeing her mother ill before.

'Mum, you shouldn't have got so fussed about it!' she exclaimed. 'I'm sane and level-headed – don't you trust me?'

She looked round the small bedroom with its familiar contours. Built-in cupboards made by the boys – all of them keen carpenters as well as sportsmen – and the sensible dressing-table, with the familiar brush and comb and tin of talc. Linda's mother, like herself, used very little make-up. Nothing in this room was superfluous. There had never been enough money for extras.

The very spartan quality of the room brought Linda down to earth, and already the excitement and fun of her holiday seemed to have ebbed away, lost in the days behind her. Now, so far as Linda could see, there was just a lot of hard work ahead, and no need for her mother to worry at all.

'You don't understand, Linda,' her mother

said, as if sensing the trend of Linda's thoughts. 'You're my only girl. It wasn't so bad, just having the boys. Boys can take care of themselves. But you're a very pretty girl, and you don't seem to be aware of it. That's what worries me!'

'What do you want me to do, Mum? Waste all the money I earn on silly clothes and cosmetics and hair sets?' Linda asked bluntly, with a wide grin to soften her words.

Her mother shook her head worriedly.

'There you go, you see! Making a joke of it all! I suppose you just can't understand why I should be taken so ill like this. But there we were – all happy at you getting a good seaside holiday for once, with very little expense, staying with your Aunt Mary – and then this blow descends on us.'

'*What* blow? All you had to say was that you'd think it over,' Linda said, surprised and exasperated.

'No, you just don't see,' her mother protested. 'We had no idea you'd go in for a competition. Well, that's all right. Just for fun, at the seaside. But then you went and won it – all that money! – and there was the televising and all these people taking you around to smart hotels, turning your head. When I saw you on television it was as if I was struck a mortal blow!'

'Oh, go on, Mum,' Linda protested. 'I don't believe it!'

'Yes, it was like a premonition of things to come. I've got the feeling that you'll be leaving us and living in a world of smart people and money splashed around and all sorts of goings-on–'

'Now, Mum, really–'

'But I wouldn't mind so much. I want you to get ahead. The trouble is, you don't seem to – well, know what it's all about.'

'I don't know what you mean, Mum. It's all right.'

'Other mothers have always said how lucky I was to have a girl who was just keen on swimming and didn't bother her head about boys and all that. Now, I don't know. I'm out of my depth.'

'What's that got to do with it?' Linda asked sharply, very much on the defensive when it was suggested that she wasn't sophisticated. 'Are you trying to tell me, Mum,' she went on, 'that I'd have my head turned by being taken up by these people? Because if you are, then forget it. I'm not a fool, you know. Besides, it simply won't arise. I haven't had a chance to tell you yet, but Uncle Zacchary has suggested a career for me that strikes me as much more interesting than anything I've heard from the others.'

'And what's that?' her mother enquired, quickly.

'He wants me to train for the swimming events, Olympics and all that. I've agreed, because that's what I want more than anything. Straight swimming. So that ought to put your mind at rest.'

'It certainly does, lovey. I just wanted you to know the real reason why I got taken sick like this. It was a bad shock, that girl coming and warning us, and we didn't like the look of that man – Tim Ripley his name was – who came from someone called Welman. It struck us – your uncle and me – that they were just on the lookout for pretty girls, to exploit them. Well, we love you too much to let you get taken up, and your life made a hash of.'

'Well, just don't worry about me,' Linda said, kissing her mother. 'You just rest up now, and get better.'

She got off the bed and straightened the sheets, talking all the time, briskly, cheerfully.

'The holiday was fun while it lasted, but now I'm back to the grind, and I don't mind a bit. Uncle's got a plan – I'm to get another job, cashier or clerk or something, that doesn't start till nine o'clock – a sit-down job. He thinks he knows someone who'll help in that direction. Then I can have an hour's practice at the Baths every day before work.'

'But you'll get a bit of a break sometimes, won't you, lovey?' her mother asked anxiously.

'Oh, you worry too much, Mum. Well, Uncle doesn't want me to go into crowded, stuffy places like cinemas, and he wants me to turn in early at night, but I shan't mind that. I can still get the odd hockey game or tennis according to the season. And there are country walks. Plenty of things to do by way of a break and also help the training.'

'It doesn't seem much fun to me, for a young girl with good looks,' her mother remarked anxiously.

'Oh, what an old worrier you are!' Linda laughed. 'I'm fancy-free, so what does it matter? There's nothing I have to think of now, except training for the first event Uncle's got in mind for me. Oh, there is one thing, though – I must write and tell Andy.'

Her mother was at once on the alert.

'Who's Andy?'

'A young man called Andy Blane,' Linda explained. 'I met him at Shenstone Bay.

He's all right. Aunt Mary saw him and approved.'

'That's nothing to go by!' her mother retorted. 'Your Aunt Mary approves of every good-looking young man. She's no more sense than she was born with, where men are concerned.'

'That's not fair, Mum. I like her. In any case, I'm only going to write and tell Andy I shan't be going through with what he had in mind for me. I'll tell him about Uncle Zacchary's training, and he'll understand.'

'What had he got in mind for you?' her mother demanded, struggling up in bed again.

Some inner instinct warned Linda not to disclose to her mother what direction Andy's grandiose plans took. There was no point in upsetting her mother any further and, anyway, she herself wasn't thinking any more about Andy's plans. It was all finished.

So she said, 'He's very vague. I think he just liked spending his holiday with me. We had fun. Now he's going back to work, like me.'

'What does he work at?' her mother insisted.

'In an office,' Linda said, firmly. It was true. She hadn't much idea of what a variety agent's office was like, but it was enough for her to say it was an office. To Linda, it no longer mattered. She had quite liked Andy but she hadn't been all that upset at not seeing him to say goodbye.

She wrote a short friendly letter to him that night, explaining just what had happened regarding Tim Ripley's visit, the girl's visit and warning, her mother's subsequent collapse and later anxiety, and her uncle's plans for her. Finishing by saying how sorry she was not to have been able to say goodbye to him, she closed her letter and went to post it.

For Linda that was the end. She didn't suppose she'd hear any more of Andy. He would see there was nothing in it for him and he'd look for some other girl to push up that ladder he was always talking about.

Any other girl might not have disclosed so much in the letter but Linda saw no reason why Andy shouldn't be given the complete picture.

Andy received the letter some days later, after it had been forwarded from his hotel at Shenstone Bay to his office in London.

He read it with rising anger. He had been very angry to find that Linda had just packed up and gone home because of a telegram about her mother's illness. Even her aunt's kind explanation hadn't assuaged his anger. He felt he had been pushed aside.

Now, in this letter from Linda – this cool, friendly letter – he saw he had been given the brush-off. He didn't even believe that Linda's mother had been taken ill. No, he reasoned, it was all because of Max Welman cutting in. How like him! Andy knew all about the big-shots like Max Welman.

As Andy saw it, Max Welman's man, Tim Ripley, had upset Linda's family, so they had pulled out, and thought up this idea of Olympics for Linda. It was all very well for them, he fumed. They'd got the brilliant swimmer. They would cash in on her swimming prowess themselves. He himself was cut out.

The details that Linda gave him of the girl who had called on them, fretted him. Caroline Chadwick. He knew that name but, for the moment, he couldn't place it.

He let Linda's letter lie fallow for a couple of weeks. He had his job to do but in his spare time he contacted people in order to discover who this Caroline Chadwick was. There might be something in it for him if Max Welman had really treated the girl badly.

Andy had small-fry contacts all over the

place and one of them worked in one of the London newspaper offices.

'Mick, I've got something here,' he confided to his newspaper friend one evening. 'Can you give me any dope on a girl called Caroline Chadwick? I know the name vaguely but I can't place her. Probably a beauty queen or something like that – taken up a year or two ago and then dropped. Does it convey anything to you?'

'Caroline Chadwick,' Mick mused. 'No, not a beauty queen. The only Caroline Chadwick I know of is the one in Max Welman's life.'

'Max Welman!' Andy ejaculated. 'Are you sure?'

'Yes, let me think. Yes, her name's Caroline. She's Joe Chadwick's only daughter. Very thick, the Chadwicks and Max Welman. Old Joe gave Max his chance when he was young and raw – gave him the helping hand, d'you see?' Mick grinned. 'More than Welman's life is worth not to hitch up with the girl, I'd say, if she wants him. And from what I hear, she wants him all right! Here, wait a tick – I've just remembered,' and Mick rifled through some photographs in a folder and found one of Max Welman at a West End party with Caroline Chadwick hanging on his arm, her father just behind.

'Let me have a closer look at that,' Andy said. 'Yes, what a mug I've been. Here, listen to this for a story,' and he repeated to his friend Mick what Linda had written in her letter about Caroline's visit and warning. 'What does that suggest to you, old son?' Andy finished.

Mick raised his eyebrows. He was a very hard-bitten young man.

'I'd say that Max Welman was after taking up your little mermaid but Caroline wasn't having any so she queered the pitch in her own friendly little way.'

'That's what I think,' Andy murmured.

'Leaves the way open for another bright promoter, if Max Welman's out of it, doesn't it?' Mick asked, looking at the ceiling with an elaborately casual air.

'Me, for instance,' Andy suggested, and Mick nodded.

'I'm thinking that, too. I'd need help. Want to come in on it from the publicity angle?'

'Brother, I'm there already,' Mick said, with alacrity. 'You know, I can flash a pretty camera as well as wield a nifty pen!'

'I know,' Andy said, coolly. 'But remember, it's my show. Get me?'

'I get,' Mick assured him.

Andy went back to his digs and wrote a carefully worded letter to Linda. 'I know how worried and upset about your mother you must have been,' he told her. 'But I did rather think we were friends. I understand how you want to please your uncle, too, with his entering you for straight contests, but that doesn't mean I can't come and visit you sometimes, does it? I'm not the sort of chap who only wants a girl for what he can get out of her. Sometimes I like a girl for herself and that's how it is with you, honey. But you're the boss – if you want to push me out of your life, like an old glove, just ignore this letter and I'll understand.'

He read it through again, and frowned. Linda was shrewd. She might well see through that, laugh and throw it into the waste paper basket and he'd never know whether she did receive it, or whether those wily relatives of hers had come on it first and stopped its progress. So he altered his letter to read:-

'So, if you don't want to see me again, do me a favour and write and tell me, man to man. You know – all this bluntness you're so proud of.' That ought to get Linda on a tender spot, he reasoned. He added, for good measure, 'I'm being transferred to our

Birmingham office next week, and I see from the map that I'd only be ten miles away from you, that's if you did decide to see an old pal again.'

From what he knew of Linda she'd feel mean if she didn't give him the chance of seeing her just the once, and – well, the rest was up to him.

When the letter reached Linda she had been in her new job for two weeks. It was the cash-desk of a sports' gear shop and Linda liked it very much. She had also been training at the Baths for fourteen days and her uncle was pleased with her progress.

Other people were getting interested. There was a professional coach who was trying to teach a very dull child to swim and, after the lesson was over, he usually strolled over to stand by Zacchary Ross and watch Linda's beautiful body cleaving through the water.

'That girl's a natural, if ever I saw one,' he remarked one day. 'What are you going to do with her, Ross?'

Zacchary told him, adding, 'There was a chap we didn't like the looks of, wanting to take her up, put her into films. We soon stopped that lark.'

Zacchary didn't say that the offer had come from Max Welman. Had he done so the swimming coach could have told him that Max Welman was one of the top men in the business and a fine man to deal with. But, as it was, a very fine chance for Linda slid by.

Because Linda was working so hard and so well, Mrs Ross didn't agree with Zacchary that Andy Blane shouldn't be allowed to see Linda.

'It might be very nice for her,' Linda's mother objected. 'I'd like her to get a nice boy friend, Zacchary. I'd feel safer in my mind. He could come here to tea on Sunday and go in time for her to get to bed early as usual.'

'I don't want her mind distracted from her swimming,' Zacchary protested.

'No, but if all you say is true, and you're planning to get her into International contests,' Linda's mother said, smiling, 'it might be nice to have a young man we can trust, to accompany her abroad. You won't want to have to go about all over the place with that game leg of yours, *I* know! Besides, there's your job.'

'There's his, too, if he's got one!' Zacchary growled.

But none-the-less it was arranged that Andy should visit Linda one Sunday after-noon.

Linda had forgotten how smart and smooth-mannered he was. He seemed out of place in their small house, with its homely furnishings, and her brothers were all so tough and strong compared with Andy. Only two of the boys were at home that day and it was clear, they weren't impressed by Andy's smartness.

After a difficult tea-time Linda hastily suggested that they should go out for a walk. She had to talk to Andy privately. It was hopeless in the bosom of the family, with her mother looking as if she was trying to read Andy's mind, and her uncle scowling as if he hated everything.

Once out of the house they walked down two quiet streets and across a golf course, and then it was open country. Across the fields, almost lost in the pinkish mauve mist on the horizon were the vague blocks of factories and the tall spires of chimneys, reminding them that this was just a little patch of country and that not far away was the mass of the industrial Midlands. The coast, Shenstone Bay and the Swimming Gala, seemed such a long way away to

Linda just then.

Leaning on a five-barred gate, she said bluntly to Andy, 'Well, you've seen my family and my background. You know there's nothing in it for you. Now are you satisfied?'

'Oh, what a girl you are!' he exploded. 'Here we have the first opportunity for saying a few private words to each other and you promptly attack me! Is it so strange that I should want to be friends with you, Linda?'

'Yes. I'm not your type,' she said, but she grinned.

'I adore you when you look like that,' he said, taking her face in his hands.

At his touch she stiffened and shrank back. Andy had known instinctively that it would be like this. But somehow he had to get through to her, make a stand, circumvent the solid mass of that family of hers by finding a chink in Linda's armour – if he wanted to make any money out of her in future.

He knew, too, that he had to act quickly, so he acted purely on instinct. He bent forward quickly, still holding her face in his two hands, and he kissed her.

Chapter 4

Linda had never been kissed before, and Andy knew it. Elation filled him. She was so untouched, so filled with exciting possibilities for the future, that it almost went to his head.

But that would spoil all hopes for his future. He recovered himself just in time, and gently put her away from him. 'I meant that, sweet!' he told her, quite seriously.

Her colour came and went. Emotions boiled up within her, and she didn't understand any of them. She took refuge in anger and indignation.

'You meant *what?*' she stormed. 'What did you do that for? You ought to know me by now – I don't like flirting!'

'Honey, that was as far from flirting as – as that skylark up there is far from us,' he said, searching for and finding a suitable parallel. 'That kiss was just to show you how fond of you I am, and how I mean to hang on to you, no matter how you go for me! So just cool down, and listen.'

'But you don't know me well enough to kiss me!' she said, only partly reassured. 'I told you – I'm old-fashioned. If anyone's going to prove to me that he likes me well enough to kiss me, then it's going to take time – so don't you think you can just pop into my house for Sunday tea and start kissing me the minute we get away from the place!'

'All right, all right, I quite understand, honey, and I respect you for it. I just wanted to stake my claim, that's all, because although I'm going to be transferred to the Birmingham office, I shan't have all that much time to come over here and keep an eye on you. So don't you forget, love – you're my girl! I'm a chap who makes up his mind on the instant and doesn't change it. I knew the minute I first looked at you, that you were my girl!'

'Yes, on the rocks above the pool, so you walked off and left me, thinking I was only a schoolgirl,' Linda quietly reminded him, with a puckering of a smile. 'It wasn't until you saw which race I was in, that you discovered I was old enough to get interested in.'

She had caught him out. He had the grace to look ashamed for a minute, and then he grinned. 'Okay, you were right there! But when I did discover how old you were, that was when I made up my mind, and even you can't deny it!'

'We'll see,' she said. She had recovered to a certain extent, but that kiss had shattered her far more than she cared to admit. Resolutely she put the memory of it behind her, and decided to make the most of their time together by convincing him that her future was mapped out as Uncle Zacchary wanted it. She told Andy, quietly and simply, just what she was working for.

'It's going to be Olympics, no matter what anyone says,' she finished, and his look of dismay and irritation wasn't lost on her. 'I myself want straight swimming, working up to the top through the Championships. I know what I'm capable of, and the first one will be the County Championships in the Spring.'

He was silent for a minute, looking down at her morosely. Then he shrugged.

'So you're just going all out for the glory of collecting cups and shields, and finishing up with very little money, in the same job as you started with,' he said, staring ahead into the distance and giving her time to think that one over.

'What's wrong with that?' she retorted. 'It's a nice job for me, and there's a whole heap of things I feel I can tackle. The Borset Brewery Shield in May, and Pevenhams the Druggists' Contest in July – they give a big money prize!'

'A few hundreds?' Andy raised a quizzical eyebrow. 'What happened to the bright plans I had for you in Shenstone Bay? Not only big money, Linda, but a glamorous life, seeing the world, meeting people, being in the lime-light. Honey, are you sure you understand what I could offer you if you put yourself in my hands?' he said eagerly, turning to her and taking her shoulders in a firm grasp.

'I don't want a lot of money, Andy, and it would only worry my mother if I was off and away with that sort of life! Look how ill she's been as it is, just with the thought of it! When that girl came and told her what sort of life she'd had–'

'Just a minute, love, you told me all that in your letter and somehow her name rang a bell,' Andy said glibly, watching Linda closely. 'Caroline Chadwick, you said, I be-lieve? Well, just listen to this. I chased up a few pals, and got the low-down on that girl. She was telling a whole pack of lies, you know!'

'Telling lies? How do you make that out?' Linda asked, knitting her brows.

'Listen, she's never been in a swimming competition in her life. She's in with Max Welman, you know. Oh, I know that bunch only too well! They're as tricky as can be! It's all a publicity stunt, and no more or less than anyone would expect Max Welman to throw. Only you honest people didn't react the right way! You believed that girl's story and cried off!'

'What were we supposed to do, then?' Linda asked, in complete bewilderment. 'Honestly, I don't know what you're talking about, Andy! All I know is, it made Mum ill at the thought of me being mixed up with anything like that!'

'Yes, I'm sorry about that, sweetie, but to be frank I don't suppose Max Welman and his pals expected to come up against anyone as good and honest as your mother! The average mother would work all the harder to see that her girl didn't come to the same sticky end! That's what your mother was supposed to do – it's an old trick to make the family more eager. Max Welman, d'you see, wants as much out of his discoveries as possible, and he's going to be darned sure the family isn't going to play greedy and get more out of it than he means them to. Oh, I know him! You steer clear of Max Welman whatever you do!'

'It all sounds crazy to me!' Linda said frankly. 'I'd much rather stick to training for straight contests, where everything is above board and I know where I am!'

'Yes, I think it's much better for anyone like you, poppet,' Andy agreed, looking back at the cluster of small houses behind them, the nice safe little rows of houses where Linda's own home was.

His look and his remark made her feel stupid and provincial, and he also made her feel as if she would never make the grade anywhere, because she and her family were too timid to take a chance.

'I could get well known, in time!' she flashed.

He considered her. 'Yes, you might, in time,' he allowed. 'I'm just wondering if you're being a tiny bit selfish, though, aiming for the career you personally want. After all, your mother's health doesn't seem too good, and she's a widow. I should have thought you'd aim for all the money you could get! Mind you, you could aim for your straight swimming and still make a tidy bit on the side by taking on the odd evening engagement – swimming demonstrations and – but no, I know you wouldn't want to do that! Forget it, poppet!'

'Well, don't stop there, Andy, now you've started telling me!' Linda cried, stung by his shrewd reference to her mother's needs. 'What sort of evening engagement could I get? I shouldn't mind that, if I could still do straight swimming for the Championships!'

'Oh, I don't know,' Andy said doubtfully. He asked himself desperately how far he could go with her. It was essential in his own interests not to place a wrong foot now!

He must get her weaned away from that obstinate old uncle of hers, who guarded her like a dragon, but he mustn't let Linda know the truth behind his own manoeuvres. Once he did that, he would lose her for good and all!

'Well, you might be able to do it,' he went on, as if thinking it over carefully. 'But you'd have to follow my lead to the last letter! Yes, it might be all right. There's a place where you might show your paces, not so far away from here. On the London Road. I could take you in my car and get you back in time for that early to bed routine.'

'Well, what sort of place is it, and what would I have to do?' she asked eagerly.

'It's a sort of nice social club – dancing, whist drives, restaurant – and a swimming pool that would make your mouth water. And all you'd have to do would be to show what you could do in the water, while people watch.'

She looked so doubtful, he could have kicked himself for putting it like that.

'They're not hard-up, honey – if you do a few clever things in the water and show off your best dives from that wonderful high board of theirs, they'd pay you fifty pounds. Now wouldn't that be nice to put by for your mother, for a start? You don't want to be always worrying about her while you're off and away doing these contests of yours, do you?'

'Fifty pounds! I don't believe it!' she said flatly. 'No one would pay that much for a bit of swimming!'

'You don't trust me! All right, forget all about it. By the way, did you get your mother that present with the money you won at Shenstone Bay?' he asked swiftly.

Her face lit up. 'Did I not! She's got the most super washing machine and spin drier! They almost didn't fit into our little wash-house! Oh, I'll never forget her face when they arrived!'

He nodded. 'And if you weren't so selfish or scared (I don't know which) you could make quite a bit one way and another, so that you need never have to worry about your mother. Just one or two evening jobs as I've just suggested to you. Nice easy jobs, with dancing flung in afterwards, or a nice meal with me – but no! Anything out of the ordinary, that you've never thought of before, and you have to turn it down right away!'

She flushed. 'That isn't fair, Andy! If you'd told me more about it – only it does seem a bit fantastic, fifty pounds for a bit of showing off in a swimming pool!'

'It isn't a bit of showing off in a swimming pool! It's a right-down regular engagement for a brilliant swimmer, to give a water show at a country club – only if I'd said that at first, it would have scared you off anyway! They've got money and they pay big money to the right people, and in your class (with a bit of grooming and dressing-up) you'd be able to command top prices.'

'It sounds more like a night club to me,' she said quietly.

'Well, all right then, so it's a night club,' he admitted, surprised that she had seen through his story. 'It's called The White

Slipper and they have a drinking licence. You might as well know from the start what a wicked place it is!'

'Don't laugh at me, Andy!' she said, in a voice that he was soon to recognise as dangerous. 'Just be honest with me, right from the start, if you want to get anywhere with me. And give me the credit for having a bit of intelligence! I may be a bit inexperienced but I'm not a complete fool!'

'I didn't say–' he began, but she cut him short.

'I should have appreciated it if you'd said simply that there was a job going at a night club near here, a straight piece of swimming and diving for a fee of fifty pounds – that's if it's really true, and nothing else involved that you're keeping from me because you think I wouldn't like it!'

'All right! All right! How you do give a chap six of the best when he's not looking!' Andy protested, hardly knowing whether to laugh or to shake her. 'I do assure you there's nothing else involved (as you picturesquely put it) and that is the fee, so help me! And in case you think I'm hiding it, I shall expect my percentage out of that, for getting you the booking. Satisfied?'

Her impish grin broke out. 'Satisfied! Just

70

for one night, back in time for early to bed, no strings attached (either with the night club or with you!) and I'll do it. But only because I do want to get Mum a lot of other things she needs, and I admit freely that the salary from my own job will never run to it! Done!' and she held out her hand to shake on it, in the most engaging manner.

'Gosh, what a girl you are, Linda!' he said, and solemnly shook with her. 'Right, now to the details. I suppose I don't have to have any doubts as to whether we tell Uncle Zacchary or not?' he added, as an afterthought.

'Well, of course we don't tell him – or anyone else – or how can it be a surprise for Mum?' Linda expostulated.

'Okay, I get it,' he said, laughing helplessly.

In spite of Linda's attempt to drag the full truth out of him, Andy omitted to tell her that he had only just thought of the idea on the spur of the moment, and that he now had to go ahead and arrange it.

She was an unknown name, so the fee was very much less than he had grandly promised her. With an eye to the future, and persuading her to do other jobs which he hoped would rise in price, he planned to find the rest of the money himself. This he did by a loan from Mick, and by pawning his watch and ring. Other men, Andy reminded himself, had had to do similar things when they were playing for a big future and so must he. He could only hope and pray that Linda would never find out that the club wasn't paying her anywhere near the fifty pounds he had stipulated.

Meantime Linda went back to her swimming training. But the memory of Andy's kiss persistently stayed, worrying her in an odd kind of way. There were all sorts of aspects to it. Had Andy meant what he said? He was such a liar, she reminded herself. Then if he hadn't meant what he said, why had he kissed her? The memory of the kiss, and the effect it had had on her, teased and perturbed her. She hated herself for being so put out over one kiss, when other girls appeared to take kissing in their stride. Perhaps if she let Andy kiss her more, she would get used to it, and be able to put the thought of it behind her.

The thought of Andy Blane visiting her often, kissing her regularly, had such a shattering effect on her that she gulped in water and nearly choked.

Her uncle shouted at her. 'Come in, girl, and get over it!' he said wrathfully. 'What's the matter with you this morning, Linda? You're doing very badly! Aren't you feeling well?'

'I'm all right. I was just – just thinking of something else at the time,' she stuttered, getting her breath with difficulty.

'That's the last thing you should be doing! How do you expect to train if you aren't even thinking of your strokes and your breathing?'

'Look, I said I'm sorry, Uncle! It won't happen again!' she protested, flushing.

He looked keenly at her. 'I shouldn't wonder if you weren't thinking of that chap who visited you on Sunday!' he said, hitting the nail on the head. 'Your mother and your Aunt Mary may be taken in by him, but I'm not! And don't you forget it! That chap's a wrong 'n if anyone ever was!'

'A wrong 'n! Uncle, that's a terrible thing to say!' she exclaimed, climbing out, and getting a towel. 'You've no right – you don't even know him!'

Her stricken face appalled him. He didn't think she knew the young fellow well enough to care so much.

'Well,' he said, on a less harsh note, 'perhaps I didn't mean quite that. See here, lass, it's a sort of instinct one man has about another. If he wasn't a friend of yours, I wouldn't think much to him, and that's a fact! I don't mean I'd suspect him of committing a crime. Bless us, I doubt if he's got it in him to do anything really big, good or bad! That's just it. Small-time, I'd say he was. Upon my word, I think I'd have more respect for the thorough-going bounder, than the chap who just nibbles at being a wrong 'n.'

He laughed, but Linda was to remember his words, and it didn't make her any happier about having decided to keep the performance at the night club a secret. So she decided to tell him part of it.

'I'm sorry you feel like that about him, Uncle, because he did want to take me out one evening, just for an hour or two, and he knows you like me to turn in early – he promised faithfully to get me back well in time for bed! Do you want me to call it off, then?'

'No, no, you can have the odd evening out,' he said, capitulating completely before her woebegone face. 'I can trust you, lass, to keep all square, and you've no one else to go out with. I'll not keep you from every bit of fun! Maybe you'll put up a better morning performance here, if I let you off the lead a bit sometimes.'

Linda felt mean now. She had only half told him what she was going to do, and in her heart she was sure he wouldn't approve if he knew the whole truth. And yet, how was she going to make a bit of money to put by for her mother meantime if she didn't take a chance on the odd evening's paid engagement?

It didn't help, the way her mother was taking Andy's visits. Mrs Ross liked Andy. He had nice little ways that the Ross boys never thought of producing for their mother's benefit. Linda's brothers held Andy in scorn and didn't hesitate to show it.

The evening of the swimming fixture at The White Slipper should have been a happy, exciting one for Linda, but somehow she couldn't rid herself of an odd premonition that something would go wrong.

As Andy tucked her into his small car, he said, 'Well, how do you feel, honey? You haven't a thing to worry about, you know – I've fixed everything!' And indeed he had, down to the last penny promised to Linda for that evening's work.

'You're sure we'll be back in time, Andy? Uncle will never forgive me if we're not!'

'I have promised, haven't I? I can't do

75

more,' Andy grumbled. Linda, he felt, should be more appreciative of his efforts, he told himself, conveniently forgetting what he himself hoped to get out of a future handling her affairs.

'I'm sorry, Andy,' Linda said, contrite. 'How do I look? I feel as if I've been poured into this dress?'

'You look a million dollars. And wait till you see the swimsuit I've got for you – flesh pink stretch satin, with exotic black flowers all over it. And a cap like a blonde wig.'

'Andy! Was that necessary?' she protested, meaning the swimsuit, but Andy thought she was referring to the cap.

'It certainly was – you've got to look the part! I've got the Press there!' He meant Mick, who had willingly cut in on what looked like the ground floor of something big.

Linda was loud in her dismay. 'Oh, you never have! What will Mum say? And Uncle Zacchary?'

'Hold your horses, honey! They're not likely to know unless you tell them. You're billed as "Lanine, Continental swimming star". How's that? Well, if you're a hit, as I think you will be, you must have a suitable handle!'

Linda felt sick. The duplicity was mounting, and it was all her fault. But if she had told her uncle, he would have said no out of hand, and she would never have had another chance. Andy certainly wouldn't have tried to get her another engagement, and, as he had pointed out, if she wanted money for her mother, this was the way to earn it.

Chapter 5

From the minute that Linda saw the brilliantly lit façade of The White Slipper, she knew the whole evening was wrong. It was an instinctive feeling, and if she could have possibly turned round and gone back home then, she would have done. But outside, among the other names of the entertainers for that evening, was the name 'Lanine, Continental swimming star'.

The Club had a system of billing in separate letters on a board, each letter finished in beads of coloured glass, and floodlit from below. Easy to put up and to take down. The entertainers came and went. The Club was splashing money to attract custom on this good position on the main London Road, and it wasn't very particular about its reputation so long as the tables and the bar were filled.

The pool, however, was beautiful, as Andy had promised, and not as small as Linda had feared. The changing rooms were on the first floor, approached by a small self-working lift.

On the same floor was the manager's office. The turn before Linda was a group of girls who appeared to be wearing no more than a few curled feathers and bead fringes; she changed quickly and came down in her cloak in time to see the last few minutes of their act. A very slick dancing team round the edge of the pool, their feathered reflections quite attractively echoed in the water.

Andy had promised to be sitting near, but she couldn't see him. There was a blur of faces in the darkened space where the tables were. All the light was now centred on the pool, and a spotlight on herself as she threw off her cloak. Someone announced her name and an orchestra started to play softly. Andy, who had made all the arrangements, told her it wasn't necessary for a rehearsal of swimming at the Club. She was to do so many straight dives, two stunt dives, and to time herself three minutes of what he called her 'fish play' which he had seen her do in the pool outside Shenstone Bay.

At the time, obsessed with her uncle's morning training and keeping the details of this evening a secret from her family, it had seemed all right. Now her doubts rose again. She could see herself in the many mirrors, and she hated the costume. She appeared to be without a costume: all she could see was the odd scattering of black blossoms on her body. She felt no better than those under-dressed girls who had been dancing in the feather costumes.

Furious with herself for caring, and re-minding herself that she hadn't been forced to undertake this job, she concentrated on what she was doing. Her beautiful diving got a great deal of applause, and following Andy's direction she finished her perform-ance with the music.

There was a flash, as a press picture was taken, then the lights went up, and a thunder of applause. Someone came and slipped her cloak round her. She slid her wet feet into her shoes, and took her bows. The music struck up again for the next act, and Linda thankfully fled towards the passage leading to the gilt lift.

Andy caught at her arm. 'You were great, kid, just great!' he said, but there was an odd, feverish look in his eyes, that she didn't understand, and put down to excitement. After all, this had been his idea!

'Thanks, Andy! Believe it or not, but I'm hungry!' she said, laughing.

'Never mind food,' he said sharply. 'Go and get changed as quick as you like, and meet me in the car park. Explain later!' and he gave her a little push, in the direction of the lift.

Shrugging, Linda hurried on. What on earth could have happened to make him want to leave here so soon? He had promised her a meal and some dancing, now her act was over!

She clutched her cloak closely round her, and pressed the lift button a second time, but it wouldn't come down. A voice said behind her, 'Shall I try? It's a temperamental little beast, this lift, and they have no stairs!'

She looked round to find a very tall young man, with dark hair that was beginning to turn silver at the temples. A most distinguished young man, with the nicest smile Linda had ever seen.

'Ah, here it comes,' he said, and as the lift came to a halt, he pulled back the doors and waited for her to enter. 'I'm going to the manager's office,' he said, and he followed her into the small space and closed the lift doors.

After a bit of persuading, the lift began slowly to climb.

'That was a very nice performance of yours,' the young man said. 'Oh, by the way, do you speak English?'

Linda forgot that she was supposed to be Lanine, the Continental swimming star, and said quite naturally, 'Yes, of course. Why?' Then the way he smiled and raised a quizzical eyebrow made her remember and she clapped a rueful hand to her mouth. 'Oh, now I've let the cat out of the bag. Anyway, I expect everyone guesses it's just a stage name.'

The young man frowned. 'Just a stage name! What is your real name, then? I think I may know it! I felt when I first saw you in the spotlight that–'

The rest of his words were lost, as the sluggish moving little gilt lift lurched to a halt half-way between floors.

'Oh, no!' Linda moaned. 'Don't say it's jammed!'

'I'm afraid it has!' the young man said, with suppressed anger. 'This isn't the first time it's happened! Oh, well, not to worry. We'll just have to wait till the last act finishes. They'll soon discover what's happened when they try to reach their dressing-rooms. It's no use shouting – the orchestra's making far too much noise.'

He leaned back against the wall of the lift, and folded his arms over his chest. 'What did you say your name was?'

Linda flushed. 'I didn't, and if you don't mind, I'd really rather not disclose it. You see, the person who – well, my manager–'

'Oh, you have someone handling your act,' he said, and Linda looked sharply at him. 'May I ask who he is?'

'His name is Andy Blane. He's not very well-known, but everyone has to make a start, don't they?' She was saying all the wrong things, the sort of things Andy hated her to say, but this man was so confident, so sure of himself, and in an odd sort of way he made her feel that in Andy she hadn't made such a wise choice after all.

'Indeed they do,' he said gravely. 'But you are a brilliant swimmer, and you really need a big name to handle you, such as Max Welman.'

'Oh, Max Welman! Don't talk to me about him!' Linda said, on surer ground now. 'Andy's told me so much about Max Welman, that I wouldn't even entertain the idea of going to *him!*'

'Has he indeed? What has he told you, may I ask? I might need to profit by the information myself.'

Little warning bells rang in Linda's head, but she couldn't think why. This man was obviously one of the wealthy customers. He had said he was on his way to the manager's office. There was no reason why he should have any connection with any of the agents. Yet she was reluctant to say any more, in spite of his quality of drawing her out.

'I just wouldn't want to go to Max Welman, that's all.'

'Because you wouldn't trust him?' he smiled. He had the most magnetic smile she had seen on any man's face, and his personality was so dynamic that suddenly the lift was too small and confined for comfort. She felt hot all over, and in despair, tore off the blonde wig.

'That's right, I wouldn't trust him,' she sighed.

His eyebrows shot even higher as he looked at her dark hair, damp and crisply curling. 'Ah, yes, now I know why I thought I'd seen you before. Linda,' he mused, clicking his fingers together in impatient recalling of the rest of her name. 'I have it! Ross! Linda Ross! And you won the Carnival Swimming Gala at Shenstone Bay!'

'Oh, no!' Linda groaned in dismay. 'It was supposed to be a secret, who I was, and now I've messed it all up! Oh, please, please don't tell anyone who I am!'

'Why not?'

'Mainly because of my family. I'm only doing this because I needed the fifty pounds so badly – my mother's not in very good health, you see. I want to go in for Olympics – my uncle's training me. My family don't want me to go into the entertainment world at all! So you see, I had to do this in secret. Oh, when will this lift get working – Andy's waiting for me!'

'Fifty pounds?' the young man echoed softly. 'Is that what you think you're getting for tonight?'

'I know I am!' she said indignantly. 'Andy said so!'

'And you ... trust this Andy Blane, but you wouldn't trust Max Welman, eh?'

She looked doubtfully at him. She wasn't bothered about Max Welman, but she knew for certain that she would trust this man to the ends of the earth.

Before she could answer him, there was a jolt from above, and the clamouring of voices below that had been going on for a few minutes – presumably the last act noisily demanding service from the lift – now grew to shouting limits.

'It would seem that the lift is being coaxed into action,' her companion smiled. 'Before we part company, let me give you a word of advice. Trust your own judgment. You look a sensible girl – you don't necessarily have to believe what other people say, especially this Andy Blane!'

Andy was fuming. Linda found him out in the car park, waiting with his car unlocked, ready, it seemed, to drive off at once.

'What's the rush, Andy? I thought we were going to have dinner and dance?' Linda puffed, short of breath from hurrying once she had got out of the trapped lift.

'There was someone in there that I didn't want to run into,' he said, shortly. 'Never mind that now. Let's clear out of here. But it's all right, you know – you're booked for next week! What about that?'

'Do you really mean that?' Linda gasped, as Andy gave his attention to backing out.

When they were on the road again, he remembered how he had had to wait for her. 'What on earth kept you, Linda? You were ages getting changed!'

'The lift got trapped half way,' she said.

'Good grief! Were you scared, in there all alone? Why didn't you call out? What happened?'

'I wasn't in there alone. A man got in at the bottom and he said it would be all right when the next act wanted it – they'd get someone to do something to it, and that was what happened. I couldn't help it, Andy – the man said there wasn't a staircase, anyway!'

'Well, thank goodness you weren't hurt,' he said, and to Linda's relief, he didn't ask any questions about the man. She was curiously reluctant to tell Andy what that stranger with the tremendous personality had suggested to her about Andy.

'Where are we going?' she asked.

'There's another place where we can eat, and still get back to your home in time,' he said.

'But why go somewhere else, just because there was someone you didn't want to see?' she asked, blankly. 'It's such a shame – the restaurant looked nice. Who was it, anyway?'

'Someone who might have recognised you,' Andy said. 'I thought you didn't want anyone to know what you were doing, seeing how your family felt about it.'

'Oh. Oh, I see,' she said, in a small voice, remembering how she had disclosed her identity to the man in the lift. 'Oh, well, never mind, it's nice going to lots of places. You do know your way around, Andy, don't you?'

'Like I'm always telling you, baby, you put your trust in old Andy and we'll go places,' he told her, laughing.

She couldn't laugh with him. The word 'trust' was unfortunate. It reminded her of what the stranger had asked her. Did she really trust Andy? And there was that odd thing the stranger had said about the fifty pounds she had disclosed that she was being paid for tonight.

'Have you got the money, Andy?' she asked suddenly.

'What money?' he countered.

'The fee, for tonight!'

'Oh, now be your age, Linda! That will come by cheque, probably tomorrow, to me, as your agent, and I will take my percentage from it, and give you the rest. You little chump, what did you think would happen? That they'd pay you out in pound notes over the counter before you said goodnight – really, Linda!'

'I suppose so,' she said. 'You forget I've never done anything like this before. And I can't help feeling it's an awfully big fee for someone no one's heard of before. Besides, why didn't I have an audition, or a rehearsal? That's what I can't get over!'

'What's eating you now, Linda?' Andy

asked, between his teeth. 'You know you couldn't have managed a rehearsal even if they'd wanted one.'

'No, but I can't help feeling like someone roped in on the spur of the moment as a stand-in for someone billed as "Lanine, the Continental swimming star!",' she said, laughing shakily.

It had been a sort of weak joke, because she was all uncertain again and not very happy. But it had a curious effect on Andy. He jerked the wheel, as if startled, and they almost ran into the kerb.

'Look out, Andy!' Linda exclaimed.

'It's all right,' he said impatiently. They were at a junction, and he seemed at a loss to know which way to go. Impulsively he turned to the right, but a few yards further on he realised they had struck a secondary road where there were no lights.

'Oh, damn, I've taken the wrong turning!' he said wrathfully. 'Why do you have to keep on and on, Linda? You take my mind off the driving!'

'I'm sorry, Andy, but it's no use blaming me for this. You should have looked at the signs first!'

'You just keep on nagging at me. Why can't you take my word for it that the thing's all right? What am I your manager for? Oh, now where are we? It's too narrow to turn – I'll just have to keep straight on and hope it picks up the main road further up.'

'Can't you back up to the crossroads again?' she asked, intending it for a helpful suggestion.

Andy snorted. 'Can't you see the headlights of at least two other cars on our tail, Linda, to say nothing of a deep ditch on each side? Have a bit of sense!' He was now thoroughly put out.

Linda sat still and quiet, and suddenly she was aware of a deep sense of danger.

'Slow down, Andy,' she breathed, peering ahead.

'Why? What's the matter now?' he demanded.

'I don't know. I can see something – something big in front of us. What is it? Put on the big headlamps. Look out!' The last two words were torn from her.

'My stars, it's a tree across the road!' Andy shouted, standing on his brakes.

Linda didn't want to go through another ten seconds like those. The tearing sound of the brakes, the sudden looming up of that big tree-trunk in their headlights, blocking their way, Andy's tension and his startled voice – all these were nothing to the sheer horror of the cars behind braking, just seconds too late. Linda took the jolt as the one behind hooked under Andy's rear bumper. The car behind him wasn't so quick at braking and crashed right into him. There was a sound of breaking glass, its tinkling as it fell into the road, and then a sudden awful hush.

Andy tore open his door and almost fell out, Linda after him. Other people spilled out from their cars. Someone ran to stop further cars coming up the road at speed. Just for a little while all was chaos and shouting.

Then one of the men took charge. An older man, less heated than Andy; he discovered that no one was hurt, that there was a callbox a few yards down the road, and that the last car was small enough to back along and turn without difficulty. This driver he persuaded to go back and get help.

Meantime, police arrived and someone organised tackle to be fetched from a garage. The elm had fallen on land belonging to a local farmer. Someone knew him and fetched him. Sixty minutes of furious activity reduced the mess.

Linda stood helplessly by, terribly aware of

how time was now running out. At first there had been good time for her and Andy to find another place to eat, and still get back home. Now they would only just manage it if Andy's car could get free, but the bumper was still locked with the car behind him. She went to find Andy, but he impatiently shook her off.

She ventured to put her problem to him. 'Uncle said I was to be back, in time for early bed,' she said.

Andy put his hands on his hips. 'Good grief! Are you still on about your bedtime, Linda, when I'm in this mess? Look at my car! Heaven knows what that bill will cost, and who'll be responsible for it! And how do you think I'm going to get out of here – climb over the tree?'

She flushed. 'Andy, I know all that, but I wondered if you'd mind if I walked back to the crossroads and got a bus or a taxi or something. I don't want any trouble at home.'

Andy felt something snap in him. He was worried and scared. He had to have this car for his job. He had mortgaged every penny he had to pull this bluff on Linda tonight. Somehow he had to find the same amount of money to cover the engagement next week, though he had managed to force up the fee a little because the manager was so pleased with Linda's performance. But this on top was just too much.

'No, you stay here with me!' he said between his teeth. 'What do you think your uncle will say if I let you go home alone? Besides, it was your fault – if you hadn't kept me waiting, we could have got away sooner, before this tree fell, probably!'

Linda was shocked and equally angry. 'We might probably have been crushed under it!' she retorted. 'Anyway, I told you, it wasn't my fault. I was trapped in the lift! It would have been perfectly horrible if that man hadn't been in it with me. He kept talking to me, taking my mind off it, and he told me we'd be free when the others came along – I wouldn't have known that if I'd been by myself.'

'Who was this chap in the lift with you? One of the waiters?' Andy asked belligerently, ready to pick a quarrel with her over anything.

'No. I think he must have been one of the wealthy customers. He looked – oh, he looked as if he knew where he was going,' she said, that being the only choice of words she could find to describe the man. She could still feel excitement race through her as she remembered him.

Andy was very still all of a sudden. He looked a little like he had looked when he was waiting at the car for her tonight, back at The White Slipper. Linda didn't understand it. 'What's the matter, Andy?' she asked slowly.

'What did he talk to you about?' he asked her. 'Tell me everything.'

'Oh, he just said that I'd put up a very good performance.'

'What else?' he insisted.

Now Linda was wary. Warning bells rang in her head again, but this time she knew why. She knew by instinct that Andy would be very unpleasant if he knew that she had disclosed so much personal information to a complete stranger.

'What's the matter with you, Andy?' she demanded, turning the whole thing back on him. 'Why do you want to know every item of small talk between me and a perfect stranger stuck in a lift? If anyone ought to know the answer to something, it's me – just who were you so anxious not to run into, at The White Slipper tonight?'

Chapter 6

Andy was angry and tired. Careless of his words. He laughed shortly.

'All right, if you must know – *Max Welman!*'

'Max Welman!' Linda exclaimed. 'He was there? Tonight?' Puzzlement, excitement, suspicion, jostled in her mind.

Her racing thoughts showed plainly in her face. Now the thing had been said out loud, Andy could have kicked himself.

With his usual slick way of talking himself out of a difficult situation, he said quickly, 'I wanted you to avoid an awkward situation if I could. The chances were you hadn't seen him – there were plenty of elderly men with bald heads and thick-lensed glasses in that place tonight! – but I knew for sure that he would have seen and remembered you, even with that blonde wig on. Well, you've had enough upsets at home through the interference of *that* man, so I did the best I could on the spur of the moment, and rushed to get you out of there. I thought it would be better for all concerned if you didn't have to meet him face to face.'

It was more successful than he had hoped, because Linda fastened on his description of Max Welman. 'Elderly! Bald with thick-lensed glasses!' she repeated, disappointment keen in her voice. 'Oh, is that what he looks like?'

Andy nodded. Without telling a direct lie, he had at least given a false impression, a deliberate false impression. But this was no time for scruples, Andy told himself firmly. It was now or never, if he was to pull himself out of his difficulties this night.

'Well, Linda, honey, you know what you're like! I did what I thought was best, because I knew jolly well that if he came up to you and announced who he was, with the intention of having another go at you, you'd probably lose your temper and lam into him, on account of what he did to your mother! (Well, if he didn't do it himself, his stooge Tim Ripley did, didn't he?) And I know you think the world of your mother, honey.'

She nodded miserably. He was right there.

She couldn't have said why she was miserable. For a moment she had harboured the wild hope that that wonderful man who had talked to her in the lift might have been Max Welman but of course, if the well-known promoter was bald and elderly and wore glasses, then it couldn't have been.

Andy waited, anxiously, watching her. He still wasn't happy about just who she had met and talked to in the lift, but it wouldn't have been Welman, that was clear, or she would have blurted it out before now. He thought he knew her well enough. But could it have been Tim Ripley? Both he and Welman had been there tonight – Andy had seen them, though he wasn't going to say so to Linda now. Instead, he said gently, 'Well, who was the cavalier in the lift? What did he look like? Or are you going to keep it a secret?'

He held his breath and waited, but he had probed too far. Linda didn't want to talk about it any more. She lost her temper.

'Oh, for heaven's sake, Andy, leave it alone! I told you – he was just an ordinary man, nice and kind, but that's all! Why all the interest in him?'

'Oh, well, I saw a red-headed chap going towards the lift and I just wondered–' Tim Ripley was red-headed, and Andy had to know – he just had to *know*.

'No, he didn't have red hair, and if you can't drive me home, then I'm afraid I must really go and try to get a lift. Be fair, Andy –

I did say that I must be home at a certain time, and that didn't allow for accidents. I just don't want another upset at home – you said so yourself, and that goes for making Uncle wild about the way I keep my promises. I'm sorry, Andy, but there it is.'

She meant it. He watched her as she hurried away. She was soon lost in the crowd milling round the wrecked cars, the tackle trying to move them apart, and the police. He had lost her, he told himself, in despair.

He clenched his fists, and surveyed what had been his serviceable little car. He dare not leave it at the moment.

He looked at the time. No matter what sort of lift Linda got now, she would be late home. Perhaps it was as well that he hadn't gone with her, for that way he would be connected with her lateness. As it was, he might yet be able to talk his way out of any liability, with that tough old uncle of hers. Linda wouldn't blame him, he was sure, when it came to explaining her lateness to her family.

With a gleam in his eyes, he turned back to his car, and stood there thinking; thinking of ways and means, not only of getting back where he had been with Linda and her family, but of getting out of the mess with his car, his shaky finances, the fee he had to find for Linda next week. And next week, he promised himself, he would see to it that Linda was not exposed to any other agents who might be around.

Linda had a long walk before her, all the way back to the main road. Her shoes weren't made for country walking, and just before she reached the crossroads where she and Andy had taken the wrong turning, her heel came off.

But here her luck changed. A police car pulled up by her as she stumbled, and when she explained her predicament, they offered her a lift home. It wasn't so far, after all, in a car, but by bus, she would have been lucky to reach home under an hour and a half.

'It's awfully kind of you,' Linda stammered, as they reached the end of her road. 'I wonder if you'd drop me here and let me limp home – you see, my mother's not too well and seeing a police car draw up, might give her a shock.'

The kindly sergeant agreed, but he did say anxiously, 'You sure you're all right, miss? You look a bit white – you should have let 'em take you to hospital with the others to get looked at. Shock can do funny things!'

'No, we were in the first car and we didn't crash. My boy friend managed to stand on his brakes in time to avoid the tree,' she explained. 'He had to stay behind until they could get his car freed, otherwise he would have brought me.'

Not till the police, satisfied, drove away, could Linda breathe again. She couldn't tell the kindly officers that their neighbours would all be gossiping by morning if they saw Linda brought home in a police car. But that was the truth, and her mother would have been the first to point it out to her.

As it was, all the lights were on, and all her brothers had been out looking for her. Her uncle was furious, and her mother had had to go to bed with aspirin and hot milk.

'Where have you been, Linda?' her uncle demanded, before he had shut the door behind her.

'Well, if you'll just let me explain, there was a bit of an accident.'

'There, you see! I knew it!' her elder brother said.

'Didn't like the look of that chap from the first!' the second one put in.

'Where is he, I should like to know?' her uncle asked, in a terrible voice.

Her mother came downstairs. Mrs Ross looked white and ill, with blue rings under her eyes, and her hair all untidy. She clutched her dressing-gown to her, and said, in a shaky voice: 'Is that our Linda?'

'Now look, it isn't all that late!' Linda fumed. 'I know I promised to be back by ten, but circumstances were against me! Let me explain!'

'Where is that fella who took you out?' her uncle repeated.

'Standing by the side of his car, in the lane where it happened,' Linda said patiently.

'In a lane!'

'Look, will you all let me tell you just what happened? We took a wrong turning – it was my fault, I was talking to him and he missed the right road – there was a tree blown down, but he managed to pull up within inches. But other cars behind us couldn't pull up, and they all bashed into the backs – about five, and we couldn't move!'

'You might have been killed!' her mother cried.

'No, Mum, it wasn't as bad as that! Just unfortunate,' Linda expostulated. 'If I hadn't promised to be back by ten, you need not have known a thing about it.'

'Oh, so you wouldn't have let on, eh?' her

brothers chorused.

'Not if I thought it would upset Mum,' Linda said steadily.

'How did you get home then, if he's still with his car?' her brother George demanded, suspicion all over his face.

'I started to walk back to the bus route, when my heel broke, so I was lucky enough to get a lift–'

'A lift! In some stranger's car!' her uncle thundered.

'No, in a police car, if you must know!'

'No car pulled up outside here,' her brother Tom said, in an odd voice. 'We would have heard it.'

'Besides, they would have brought you to the front door,' Donald put in, frankly derisive. Donald was the youngest and the hardest to convince about anything.

'I thought it would upset Mum to see a police car so I asked them to drop me at the end of the street and they did. Look, I'm sorry I'm late home but it wasn't my fault. I did my best–'

'Why didn't you phone the shop on the corner to bring a message?' Tom put in. 'You could have done that, if there really was an accident.'

'What d'you mean – *if there really was an*

accident?' Linda echoed. 'Don't you all believe me?'

She looked from one to the other of them, but they were all looking at her damaged shoes, and at her frock, which had a split from the neck down, which must have happened when that branch caught at her, in the darkness of the lane, when they first tumbled out of the car. She forgot that the family hadn't seen these clothes before, and that she had bought over-smart things, not her style at all, with the special requirements of the evening in view.

'Where did you get those clothes?' her uncle asked, in an awful voice.

'I bought them, out of my own money!' Linda flared.

'They're in a bit of a mess,' George commented.

'Well, you can't expect not to damage your clothes in a narrow lane, with trees over-growing, in the confusion of an accident,' Linda retorted. 'Look, for goodness' sake, I'm tired, and we're all upset. Let's leave it till the morning.'

'I think you ditched that chap,' George said furiously, 'because you bit off more than you could chew, and when I find him I'm going to punch him right in the nose!

And you got a lift home and that's why you didn't let the people come right up to our door! That's what I think!'

'But there *was* an accident! You'll see it in the papers in the morning!'

'I'm not saying there wasn't an accident, Linda, but you weren't involved. You just used it as an excuse because you were afraid to tell us the truth!'

Her mother started crying, and her uncle began to storm at her. Linda got up.

'If that's what you all think, then it means you don't trust me, and that's the finish. How can I go on living here, working for all Uncle has dreamed up for me, if this is how you're going on? If you won't even take my word—'

'You haven't told us where that Andy was taking you in the first place yet, Linda,' her mother sobbed, mopping at her eyes. 'I did think you'd be honest about that!'

Linda turned round and faced them all. 'I've been swimming tonight, for a fee. For Mum, to get her a few things. Andy fixed the engagement. It was a good one. And it was to be a lovely surprise. Lovely surprise! That's good, looking at the way it turned out!'

They were silent, before this piece of news.

'How much was the fee?' George asked, finally.

'Fifty pounds.'

'Fifty pounds! You must be crazy if you think we're going to believe that!' her brothers cried in unison.

She explained about it, carefully, leaving out the bits she thought would only lead to further dissension. 'I bought these clothes, because we were going to have dinner there afterwards. I shall have to look nice if I'm going to be seen around,' she said reasonably, but keeping her voice even was difficult. She was deadly tired now, and worried; the strain was beginning to tell on her, and this row on top wasn't making things any easier. 'I've left the new swimming costume in Andy's car so I can't show you it to prove it. But at least I can show you the cheque – less Andy's legitimate commission – when it arrives. The day after tomorrow, he thought. Now, if you've finished questioning me, I'd like to go to bed. Goodnight, all!'

'Just a minute, Linda,' her uncle said. 'All right, so that's your story; you had an engagement, you wanted to make some money for your mother. That sounds all right. I suppose we could check on it to prove it. But that much money for you – unknown – no, I just can't believe that, Linda. I'm not saying you're at fault, but there's been monkey business somewhere and I intend to find out where!'

Linda whitened. First that man in the lift querying the size of the fee, and now her uncle. Could they both be wrong? Come to think of it, it *was* an awfully big fee, but Andy had been so convincing.

She felt cold inside her and when she was in her bed at last, that night, going over the whole unfortunate scene in her mother's sitting-room again, she promised herself that she, too, would go into the size of that fee, the next morning.

They had all cooled down, by the time Linda joined them at breakfast. There was not likely to be much said, at that time of the day.

One by one her brothers swallowed their food and the scalding hot sweet tea their mother never failed to have ready for them, and they hurried away from the house. George on his motor-bike, Tom in their neighbour's van, and Donald half running, half walking, to the nearby bus-stop.

'I'll not be giving you your hour at the baths this morning,' Linda's uncle said briefly. 'We're none of us fit for it. We'll see how things are for tomorrow,' and with nothing more than a brief nod, he left them.

Linda looked uneasily at her mother across the breakfast table and hoped devoutly that her mother wouldn't insist on going over it all again, just because the others had gone, and Linda was unusually left alone here.

'I'd rather you didn't, Mum–' she began, but her mother, with unusual firmness, cut in.

'I've only one question to put to you, lass, and I've a mother's right. I want to know – did he, last night? Was it like George said?'

Linda's face flared with angry colour, then the colour ebbed away leaving her very white. 'You could ask me that, Mum? You?'

'It's been known before, with the nicest girls,' her mother said. 'I just want to know the truth, lass.'

'Well, you've had the truth! Last night! If you must know, there was nothing further from Andy's mind, or mine! And furthermore, if you must know, we were quarrelling almost the whole time, about you and Uncle! There! Satisfied?'

Her mother saw she had gone too far, but she had done her best and what she thought was right. 'Quarrelling? About your uncle and me? What on earth for, I should like to know! We let you go out, didn't we?'

'Yes, you let me go out, without any leeway for something like that happening, and not even believing me when I came back and told you the whole truth. I didn't have to tell you all about the swimming – I could have kept that a secret. I wanted to, but I didn't. You, all of you got the whole truth last night, even to the amount of the money, and you wouldn't believe me. That hurt so much. I don't think I'll get over that in a hurry!'

She left the house then, for fear any more should be said by either of them that they would be sorry for.

Somehow she must find a way of convincing them all that what she said was true. But even when she did, what then? What would happen when she went out with Andy again – if she wasn't prevented from going!

She couldn't give her mind to her work that day. All she wanted was the post next morning, with Andy's letter and his cheque, so that she could show it to them all.

But even then, she only had Andy's word for it. She might have believed it herself, but she was quite sure her family wouldn't. Even her mother, who had liked Andy and stuck up for him, seemed to have gone off him now, convinced as she was that he and Linda had merely stopped somewhere, and Linda had walked home because Andy had wanted to make love to her.

The idea was so ludicrous that Linda almost laughed aloud, but the question of the money nagged at her.

So much so that at last she couldn't stand it any longer. In her tea-break that afternoon, instead of slipping over to the café across the way, as she usually did while someone else took over the cash-desk, she went instead to a call-box and found the telephone number of the White Slipper Club.

She didn't know that the office there rarely opened until seven thirty, but as it happened, the telephone was switched through that day to the private flat of the manager, and he himself answered it.

'Look, I'm awfully sorry to worry you, but I'm the girl who swam last night in your pool – Lanine the Continental Swimming Star, remember?'

'Oh, yes, I remember,' he said, in a queer voice. 'The chick who stood in and got me out of a hole. You did very nicely, girlie. What can I do for you?'

Linda didn't take up the point about

109

standing in – that could come later. All she wanted to know about now was the money. 'Well, look, I know this isn't the usual thing to do, but I've got a special reason. My agent told me how much you were paying me, but I think I've got it wrong. It seems rather a lot.'

'How much did he say, kid?'

'Fifty pounds,' Linda faltered, convinced now that it was far too high a price.

This was absolutely confirmed by the roar of laughter at the other end. Derisive laughter, but amused laughter. He appreciated some joke which Linda didn't understand.

'You're right, baby, it does seem rather a lot, from my point of view – but perhaps not from his, eh?'

'I don't understand you, but the point is, just how much did you say you'd pay me?' Linda asked desperately.

'Now, on the level, kid, you shouldn't be doing this. But because something's going on that I don't understand either, I'll satisfy you. But first of all, just what did that smart Alec tell you?'

'No, please, really, there's nothing going on, so far as my agent's concerned. I trust him, and I could have waited till I got his cheque – I know it will take a day or two to come through, but I got the amount wrong and I feel such a fool. I don't want to bother him again. You tell me.'

'Sure, sure, if that's the way you want it. It's all one to me, if you know what you're doing. This is the way it was. Lanine's an old has-been, bless her! Too old for the job, but she's got a name on the continent, so I took her on. Obliging an old friend, if you know what I mean. Well, she broke her perishing ankle and let me down with half a day's notice. Well, I ask you! Then your agent rings up and asks if I want a swimmer. It was a gift, I tell you! Mind you, I didn't want to pay twenty quid – fifteen was my limit, I told him – but the blighter beat me up to it. I was in a hole so what could I do? What's a fiver? So there you are! I paid him in fives before he left. Now, over to you, kid! Sure you wouldn't like to come over after the show this evening and tell me all about it?'

'Thank you, but I'm afraid I'm not free. You did want me for an evening next week, to swim I mean, didn't you?'

'I didn't, but it's an idea – but not with that agent of yours. I don't like him, kid. He makes me nervous.'

'I couldn't do anything without my agent,

thank you just the same,' Linda said, and rang off.

So it wasn't true. Lanine was not her show-business name that Andy had thought up for himself. It hadn't been fifty pounds – she wasn't worth fifty, only fifteen! And there was no date for next week. It was all in his imagination.

No, not imagination, just plain lies. If he had talked it over with her first, let her know what he was doing, even then it might not have been so bad. But of course, in fairness to Andy, Linda herself wouldn't have fallen for the idea. In all honesty, she hadn't liked it. She hadn't liked the atmosphere of the club really, and she certainly hadn't liked the manager, over the telephone just now.

What would she tell them at home? What would Andy do about the cheque? Would he send fifty pounds – and if so, why? And he had had that twenty all the time, even while he was making her feel a fool for thinking that they didn't pay cash over the counter!

With scorching cheeks, she made up her mind what she must do. She would tell the family she had been a fool, misheard Andy – it had sounded like fifty, but he had been saying fifteen. Pride wouldn't allow her to show them how he had taken her in.

As for Andy, she sat down and wrote a letter to him, before she left her job for home. A brief letter. 'Don't bother to send the money, Andy. Keep it – you'll need it for your car repairs. And don't bother to contact me any more – I'm through with side plans. I'll settle for straight swimming after all.'

Chapter 7

Linda's mother watched her daughter anxiously in the weeks that followed. It had been a golden October, with the wind rushing across their small strip of countryside, taking with it the golden and crimson leaves; dry, healthy weather that Mrs Ross loved so much. November brought its quota of fogs, but none of the frosts and keen east winds that she dreaded.

Usually Linda was full of the changing seasons, and went for short walks with her mother in the weekend, but this year Linda seemed entirely preoccupied with her training. Since that affair of Andy Blane keeping her out late that night, she seemed to have turned inwards on herself.

Mrs Ross tackled the girl about it one evening. 'Is that you, Linda? Is your uncle with you?' she called, coming out into the hall bringing a trail of good cooking smells with her from the kitchen. 'Ugh! Foggy again! Come in quick lass, and get a warm by the fire. I've got soft roes on toast for you, and your favourite pudding to follow, and lots of nice hot tea.'

'I'm not very hungry, Mum, and I'm certainly not cold. Uncle and I got a lift in Mr Simpkin's van – he's still talking to him at the gate!'

'Well, he soon will get cold if he hangs about there. Never mind, I wanted a word with you, if I could get you by yourself. What are you doing for your Christmas shopping this year? I wondered if you'd like to go into Birmingham for it?'

Linda winced. Andy had been transferred to the Birmingham office, she recalled. She didn't want to risk running into him, but she didn't say so. She had avoided saying anything to her mother about him, once the subject had been closed.

'I thought I'd like to go to London, Mum, actually.'

'To London! Now that's a tidy long trip – I don't know as I could stand up to that, dear, what with the crowds and everything!'

'Well, you can't very well go with me as it's to choose a secret present for you,' Linda said, with a smile. She had actually wanted to go alone to *be* alone, but her mother wouldn't have understood that, and she would have been hurt. 'Besides, we went to Birmingham

115

last year. If you want to go shopping, how about trying somewhere else? Follington, for instance. Not such a long journey, either.'

'I see Follington once a month, regular as clockwork,' her mother protested. 'Oh, well, never mind, if you don't want me to be with you, well, you don't, and that's all.'

Linda smiled at her mother and didn't argue. Not so long ago, she would have done as her mother had hoped: begged her not to be like that, and capitulated about Birmingham. Not any more. There would have to be a time when she made a stand and didn't allow herself to be persuaded by the family to do something she didn't want to, and Birmingham was as good a subject as any to take a stand over.

Mrs Ross was a good mother, but she had never known when to stop questioning her children. With the boys it hadn't been so difficult, but Linda being a girl, she had felt especially driven to keep the girl's life an open book.

'I suppose you're afraid of running into that Andy Blane again,' she couldn't resist saying.

'That's right, Mum,' Linda agreed, composedly.

'Well, it isn't likely, is it, dear? It's a big

place, isn't it?'

'Yes, Mum. I'll just get a wash, I think.'

Her mother followed her to the sink. 'I couldn't help noticing you've had two or three letters from him since that time. Did you get the money all right – the fifteen pounds as it turned out to be after all and not fifty?'

She held her breath, hoping Linda wouldn't get angry, but Linda just smiled. 'What do you think I'm using for your surprise present, then?' was all she said. And her mother knew that it wasn't really an answer anyway.

This new Linda puzzled and distressed her. Linda was growing up too fast, and she felt she was being shut out.

'Are you going out tonight, dear?' she asked Linda. A regular question, always with a negative answer. Linda hadn't run any more risks with time, since that dreadful night.

'No. Training too hard. Uncle wants me to have a shot at the Tiverbale Club's Silver Trophy. Besides, there's my land conditioning, too. Don't want to go out at night.'

'Oh! Well, perhaps it's as well, dear. But don't feel we want to keep you in. After all, I don't mind going to the pictures with you, or you could go with one of your brothers.

A little treat might be good for you.'

'Yes, Mum,' Linda agreed, with such amenity that her mother realised she would get no further with Linda tonight.

Her uncle was pleased with her progress. 'I don't think we need worry, Margaret,' he said, after Linda had gone up early to bed, with a book to read. 'She seems content enough and since that chap went out of her life, she's given all her attention to her swimming. Don't have to tell her she isn't concentrating any more.'

'Doesn't she ever mention him? Or that swimming she went in for, at that club?' And when her brother-in-law shook his head, and appeared satisfied, Mrs Ross went on thoughtfully, 'Funny, that. I'd have thought she'd tell us what it was like, now everything's cooled down and been forgotten. Mrs Black said her girl's been there and it's a rare posh place. Lovely pool and everything.'

'Our Linda won't talk if she isn't a mind to,' Zacchary observed. Privately he thought Linda's mother would hear more if she didn't ask the girl so many questions.

'She says she's going to London shopping all by herself, nearer Christmas,' Mrs Ross went on. 'Have you said she could, Zacchary?'

'First I've heard about it, but between you and me, her training's going so sweetly that I don't intend to put her back up about anything, and I hope you won't either.'

'But you're never going to let her go all the way to London in Christmas shopping crowds, all by herself?'

'Let's put it this way,' Zacchary said, turning to his paper with a smile. 'I'm not stopping her, but it might just so happen that George or Tom will be going with the girl friend, and our Linda won't very well be able to insist on going on her own then, without it looking mighty suspicious!'

'Oh, you're a smart one, Zacchary! Well, that's put my mind at rest. I'll own I thought that Andy Blane was in this trip to London, somewhere!'

Linda went agreeably enough, with her brother Tom, and his new girl friend Tess. Tess had relations who had invited them all to stay the night, on studio couches. A pot-luck affair, Tess said, giggling. Tess was a nice girl, but empty-headed. Linda didn't find it difficult to get away from her and the infatuated Tom.

She hadn't been to London since their father had taken them on a day trip as children. Armed with a map and guide book, she had a wonderful time, and all the stresses of the past ten weeks were ironed out. She did her shopping for the whole family, with the money she had saved, and bought little presents for Tess's relatives. Then she set out to sight-see.

London was crammed with people. Only ten more shopping days to Christmas, the posters warned. Linda found herself strap-hanging on the Underground with a noisy, happy crowd of young people, and one very tall man whose eyes regarded her over the top of a girl's woolly cap. Dark hair touched with silver at the edges, and nice dark eyes that looked at her in astonished pleasure.

It was the man who had been trapped with her in the lift that night at The White Slipper!

He edged round the laughing girl in the knit cap and swinging precariously on one strap, his arm full of gaily wrapped presents, he held out his other hand to Linda. 'How are you? It *is* Linda, isn't it?'

She nodded, excitedly smiling, and with difficulty, transferred her guide books and handbag to her strap-holding hand, while she shook his outstretched one.

'How's the swimming?' he asked, and as the train swung round a corner, they were

120

thrown together, his parcels crushed between them. 'More peaceful than this train ride, I hope?'

'Yes, fine! But I love all this! It's the first time I've been to London for Christmas! Do you live here?' she asked him.

His eyebrows raised even higher at that. 'Don't you know where I live? I thought everyone knew – in the swimming world, that is!'

'Do you swim, too, then?' Linda asked him, her eyes dancing with this bond between them. 'Was that why–' She broke off in confusion. She had been going to say, was that why you were at The White Slipper. Then she could have bitten her tongue out. The least said about that night, the better!

As it happened, he hadn't noticed. Someone was struggling to get near the doors ready to alight at the next station, and he was giving his attention to the parcels he carried.

'Are you in London for Christmas?' he asked, as soon as he was able to look her way again.

'No, worse luck! Going back to Crackington,' Linda said, pulling a face. Crackington would be very dull for Christmas, after having seen Regent Street's fantastic decorative lights strung across from building to building, and all the wonderful shop windows; the light powdering of snow on Wren churches, and the river with its warehouse roofs white like frosted icing on cake-tops. 'Are you?'

'No, good heavens, no! I'm going to be in—' he began, but never managed to finish, for a beautiful blonde girl who had been sitting just behind him got to her feet, and tugged his arm.

'Darling, are you asleep? This is our station! Come on, hurry up!' she said, and didn't let go of him.

He said a hasty but rueful goodbye to Linda, shouting 'Happy Christmas!' over his shoulder, and they just managed to get through the crush before the people on the platform started pouring into the train. He lost one of his parcels and the last Linda saw of him as the train moved out of the station, he was rising from the floor red-faced but triumphant, brandishing a very large parcel wrapped in scarlet paper and gilt string. What fun he looked, she thought wistfully.

She was aware of being filled with an odd excitement; her heart was racing and tumbling over itself, and even the Underground train looked a gay wonderful place to be in. Fancy meeting him here, of all places, she said to herself. But it had been such a transient meeting. He had known her name, but she had no idea what his was, of all idiotic things!

Then she was brought down to earth with a bump, as she recalled that he hadn't been alone. He had been claimed rather imperiously by that beautiful blonde, who had been so glamorously shielded from the cold by a pale green coat and hood edged with rich dark fur. Linda looked down at her own coat; practical tweed, built for sturdiness, for getting grabbed at and caught in a rough-and-tumble journey like this, among the happy, thoughtless shopping crowds.

Taking herself to task, she got out at the next station hardly caring where it was, anxious only to be out of the Underground, leaving behind if she could, that silly dream of that handsome young man who already had a girl friend.

She wandered aimlessly out of Tottenham Court Road Tube Station, up past St Giles's Church and along Charing Cross Road. Unseeing she was jostled by the Christmas crowds – all paired off. She felt she was the only one who had just said goodbye to the one man who could lift her feet from the ground and make her walk on air … and he had another girl.

It was in Trafalgar Square that her thoughts were sharply torn away from the encounter in the Tube train. Inevitably Linda stopped to stare at people with pigeons on their shoulders, and leaning aimlessly against the side of the pond where the fountains were, a young man.

Linda stared incredulously, but it was too late for flight. He had seen her.

'Linda!' he exclaimed, coming eagerly towards her.

'*Andy!*'

'What are *you* doing here?' he asked her. 'You were the last person I expected to see, here of all places!'

'Just shopping for Christmas. Come to that, what are *you* doing here, Andy?'

'Ah, well, that's a long story. We can't talk here. Let's go and find a coffee somewhere. I know a quiet little place.'

He took her arm, confident that she would raise no protests. He didn't even ask if she was waiting for someone, she noticed with annoyance.

'I can't stay long, Andy. I'm staying with my brother's girl friend's family, and I just went out shopping for an hour or two.'

'Oh. Well, that's all right!' He looked a bit

vague, and didn't ask which brother. It didn't matter to him, she saw, searching his face. He was full up with the subject of Andy Blane, and determined to tell her all about it.

The café was a long narrow one, with big mirrors edged with stick-on advertisements for meat-flavoured hot drinks and ice creams. There was a greasy smell of cooking, coffee, fried potatoes. Linda shuddered and settled for tea.

'Why didn't you answer my letters, Linda?' he began, as soon as the tea had arrived. 'You *did* get them, didn't you?'

'Do you think my family would have withheld them?'

'Now don't sound like that! What else *could* I think?'

'Didn't you get them back? I returned them, unopened, Andy,' she said, evenly.

'Oh. Well, as a matter of fact, I've left that particular place.' He avoided her eyes, but as she said nothing, he burst out, 'Oh, well, what does it matter? You might as well know – I'm not in Birmingham any more. Not even in that firm. I got the push.'

'You were sacked? But why, why, Andy? You were very keen on your work, weren't you?'

'Keen! That's a good word. A very, very good word, Linda. So keen that I tried to push up the ladder a sure winner I found, and all I got out of it was my car busted up, and a long bout in hospital.'

'In hospital! You've been ill? But what of– I mean, how–'

'How does that connect with my car?' He smiled lopsidedly. 'You went off and left me to cope, remember? You might not have realised that it started to rain. It rained cats and dogs, and I got soaked, trying to get my car out of that mess. Well, that's all right, I suppose. Other chaps got soaked, too, in that particular mess that night. It was a long job, getting those cars unhitched.'

'You wouldn't have expected me to stay and get soaked in the rain too, would you, Andy?'

'You wouldn't have been! You'd have been inside the car! But at least I was hoping that you'd have waited with me, given me a bit of support, and then perhaps let me come into your house for a coffee or something hot. I'd had no food,' he said angrily. 'No food for hours!'

'Whose fault was that? I wanted to stay and eat at The White Slipper, not run away from someone!' she retorted. 'Oh, there we go! You see? We can't be together for five minutes without falling out. What's the use, Andy?'

'You haven't heard it all. But perhaps you don't want to.'

'All right, go on. How did you come to get ill in hospital. And why didn't they hold your job open for you?'

'A little matter of pneumonia, Linda, through a chill. I lost my car because I – well, I nipped in for a hot drink, just before closing time. I wanted warming up, but on an empty stomach – well, I suppose I couldn't see clearly and I misjudged my distance. Some idiot was overtaking at the same time. I skidded to avoid him and smashed the bonnet into a lamp post. I was thrown out. I just caught a chill,' he finished bitterly.

'Well, I'm very sorry, Andy, but you can't blame me for that. But what about your job?'

'Now that is a different matter, Linda. I lost it because a certain young lady got talking over the telephone with the manager of The White Slipper because of a fee he was supposed to have paid.'

'Oh!' She dashed a hand to her mouth. 'Well, how did it lose you your job? I only asked him – I said I thought I'd misheard you as fifty sounded a lot.'

'He made it his business to chat about it when he was doing some business with my boss, that's all, Linda.'

'Oh, that man! I didn't like him though I only talked to him over the telephone. He had no business to tell your boss! I'm sorry, Andy, but – well, even that wasn't my fault because if you'd been honest with me in the first place, it wouldn't have happened.'

'You mean, if I had told you every little detail in the first place, you wouldn't even have gone there that night! Oh, I know all that!' he said.

'You don't know anything of the kind!' she returned spiritedly. 'I told you, when I first met you, that if you played fair with me, I'd let you work on me to get me ahead. But you've never played fair with me. You try out all sorts of stories on me and if I don't catch on that they're not the truth, then you try to get away with all sorts of things! It's no good, Andy – it's got to the point that I just can't trust you any more. But I would have gone all the way with you if I'd felt I could trust you!'

He thought that over, and finally nodded. 'Yes. Yes, I know. I know all that! I suppose I knew it all the time, but I played it my way.

I've always had to. Tell the tale, convince the other chap you're better than you are, and hope you can carry the bluff all the way.'

'It isn't really necessary, Andy,' she said seriously.

'Oh, isn't it! You don't know! How could you? Cosseted and shielded by that family of yours! You've got a ready-made career, and you don't happen to want to make a lot of money, so there it is, on a plate for you. But with me, it's different. It's a whole lot different. There are too many chaps about who've been to posh schools, university – in every business, even show business. It's them that get the pick of the jobs, regardless of ability.'

'Oh, no, Andy, I can't believe that!'

'Because you don't want to believe it, Linda, that's all, because believe me, I'm speaking the truth now. Me, I've had nothing. No education, no one to give me a leg-up. I'm on my own and always have been. Well, I do the best I can, with what I've got, and believe me, it isn't much. The gift of the gab, that's all. That, and the ability to spot a winner. But winners don't grow on trees. I saw you, and I could have made something of you, if I'd been given the chance – my way, at that!'

'Sorry, Andy, but I don't like your way. I'm sure there's no need for lies, not to me, anyway. Spin yarns to other people about my ability, if you like, because I'd work to make them come true. But not tell me lies about the size of the fee, nor lies about the name you'd made up for me to appear under, when all the time there was someone else who had a right to that name!'

He had the grace to look ashamed. 'So you found that out, too, eh? Boy, that chap can open his big mouth wide!'

'He didn't go out of his way to tell me. He just happened to mention that the real Lanine had broken her ankle, and you happened to come along at that very time with a swimmer, and it got him out of a hole at short notice. I'd have understood if you'd told me that, Andy, in the first place. I'd have been grateful for even fifteen pounds – even that seemed a lot. But fifty! Well, I didn't feel I was *worth* that much!'

'There you go again, Linda! It's the wrong attitude! You've got to believe you're tops, worth the earth, if only people will believe it!'

'All right, so we've got different ideas. What will you do now? Have you got another job?'

'Another job! What, with no reference? Who's going to take me on, in a world full to busting with chaps who are convinced they can become top-line agents handling stars overnight, and who wouldn't try out funny business over fees.'

She sighed. 'Oh, Andy, I'm sorry, really I am!'

'Then prove it. Prove it, Linda, by giving me another chance! Go on, say you will! I promise you, I won't tell you another lie! Not a single one! Go on, Linda, it's Christmas time. Give me a break!'

'But how *can* I, Andy? I'm committed to Uncle's programme – I've got two contests in May and July and he's putting me down for a club shield contest in April. I'm even packing in land conditioning, as well as swimming and diving for an hour each morning and most of the weekends!'

'Just say I can represent you. That's all I ask!'

'Now wait a minute,' she said, warily. '*Why* is it all you ask? What's in it for you, Andy? What have you done?'

He dropped his eyes. 'Oh, all right, I'll tell you! I got the offer of a job because I said I could produce a star of tomorrow at the drop of a hat! (That's you! Well, I thought if

131

I could mention your name it would be all right!) Only I couldn't get in touch with you.'

'Who did you promise this to, Andy?' she asked quietly.

'The agent acting for the new panto in Follington. It's a sort of mixture of nursery rhymes with a water show – a tank on the stage. It needs a brilliant swimmer and their only hope has had a film offer and taken off. She might come back, and you'd be understudy, but either way, I'd get my old job back. Say you'll do it, Linda – it won't involve you in anything, if they get their star back. It's that or out of work for Christmas, and goodness knows how long afterwards,' he pleaded.

'All right, Andy, but this time – no more tricks,' she sighed, capitulating.

Chapter 8

Linda was committed now, but she didn't see what else she could have done. It was the thought of Christmas – happy for her in the bosom of her family, and bleak for Andy who not only had no family, but neither job nor roof over his head – that decided her.

Oddly enough, this picture swayed her mother to her way of thinking when she reached home again and told the family.

Her brothers were furious, of course. 'That chap's a real twister! He could spin any yarn and get away with it!' Tom exploded. He had been given the job of looking after his sister, and had fallen down badly on it.

'Never mind, boys,' Linda's mother said. 'In this one case I feel that our Linda did the right and proper thing. I would have done it too, if I'd been her! She's made him promise there'll be no more lies to her, and anyway, think of it – our Linda in panto!'

Zacchary looked thoughtfully at his sister-in-law. It was clear that if the bait had been any other form of entertainment than the apparently innocent field of pantomime, Mrs Ross wouldn't have been on Linda's side at all.

'All right. I see I'm over-ridden. I'll say no more, except I'm not going to stand back and let Linda get herself worn out with rehearsals. Work with me at the Baths comes first!'

Linda's feelings were decidedly mixed. She hadn't expected her mother to swing over to her side in such a way.

'Happy, dear?' her mother asked, as she came up to kiss Linda goodnight that night.

'So-so,' Linda admitted. 'Tired, though. I loved London.'

'I bet you did! Confess it now, you went with the express purpose of running into that Andy, now didn't you, love? Pity you couldn't tell your old Mum, though, before you went. I feel shut out, somehow!'

'Oh, Mum, don't be silly! Of course I didn't go to see Andy! You could have knocked me down with a feather when I ran into him in Trafalgar Square.'

'Well, dear, if that's your story, we'll say no more. I expect you want to keep your little secrets.'

Linda left it at that. Not entirely out of wisdom so much as that she was so staggered to think that her mother could jump to such a conclusion. There was safety in it, too, for while her mother held that view, she wouldn't be likely to uncover Linda's real secret; that she had met the one man for her, the man she kept meeting and didn't even know his name.

Linda's mother revealed that like Aunt Mary, they both had a weakness for young men of Andy's slender good looks and charm. Their memories were short, as to his little deceits and lies. White lies, Linda's mother said fondly, in the days that followed. White lies because he's a young man in love.

Even when the pantomime idea fell through, it didn't make any difference. Linda, however, felt she had again been let down.

'Tell me again what happened, dear,' Linda's mother pressed, when Linda came back keenly disappointed from Follington. 'I didn't know the audition was to be in a lunch-hour.'

'Neither did I till the last moment, and I'm not even sure that that wasn't Andy's make-up. The producer didn't seem to know much about it. He admitted that they'd had a bit of trouble with the girl who had first been offered the part, but the film part she had gone off for, had turned out to be small and not very well paid, so she came back at once. And they've got an understudy. Trust Andy to spin a yarn to get me to agree to help him! Wait till I see him!'

'Now don't be hasty, dear. Remember, it's Christmas. Wait till after the season of good-will is over, and then if he doesn't find something else nice for you, we'd better think again. But do you know what I think it will be? An engagement ring, dear!'

'Are you serious, Mum? I mean, do you *want* him to be engaged to me?'

'Well, don't *you* want it, too, duck? Between ourselves everyone expects it. Even your Uncle Zacchary's coming round to it! Well, not exactly coming round, but let's put it this way – he did say to me not two nights ago that if you're both going to get engaged he wished it'd happen soon, so you could give your full attention to your swimming again!'

'*Did* he?' Linda said grimly. 'Well, perhaps I'm not concentrating on my work since Andy came back into my life, but not for the reasons you think!'

'Well, you're behaving like it dear, both of you! Scrapping and making up, all glum one minute and on top of the world the next!

That's true love, if you like!'

'But I thought you couldn't stand the thought of him being around! You wanted him to go out of my life!'

'Oh, come, Linda, duck, that was only when I wasn't sure if his intentions were honourable, but now he's had a little talk with me, I'm convinced that all he wants in life is to make you a good husband.'

'Oh, so that's it! He's had another of his little talks, has he?' Linda said, understanding at once.

Still, if it meant the family leaving her alone, and giving her more freedom, she thought it might be as well not to scorn the friendship Andy offered her. But engagements were not part of the bargain, she told herself furiously.

Andy himself was most contrite about the pantomime falling through. 'Linda, honestly, love, it was about the last word! I was so furious, I could have kicked the bloke and his beastly little swimming star! But there it is – the luck of the game! Just keep your chin up and trust Andy! Now, I've got a surprise for you!'

'No, not another one, Andy! Just leave me alone to enjoy a quiet Christmas, and no surprises until afterwards,' Linda begged.

'Your surprises don't turn out well.'

'This one will, love – it's something really nice for you, to make up for the disappointment of not getting the panto date. This is a real slap-up party at a brand-new top-notch hotel, with show business in force! Lots of big names all glittering all over the place, and people to introduce you to, and fun! Fun as you've never dreamed of before!'

'What does all that mean?' Linda asked quietly. 'Two or three people having a bit of a dance at a small hotel somewhere, and you have to pay for the tickets for us?'

'Well, to be honest, the tickets are complimentary – well, not in the real sense, but they were for a chap I know and he can't go so he asked me if I'd like them. How you do cut a chap down to size, Linda!'

'Is that all the truth, Andy? No other strings?'

'No strings at all, honey, and the bit about it being a big smart hotel does really happen to be true! In Birmingham, too!'

'How do we get there, in party clothes?'

'My pal's lending me his car,' Andy said patiently. 'I'm sorry it's not my own, Linda, but you see, I didn't get a bean on mine when I smashed it up because I had had a drink (I told you, to keep out the cold!) but there it was. No one else would believe that, so it was a dead loss when I crashed it!'

She softened, as always, before his run of bad luck, and after a very quiet Christmas at home, she was glad to have the party to look forward to.

'How was it with a family of your size that you didn't have a high old time?' Andy demanded, when they were on their way to the party.

Not for worlds would he admit to Linda that he had been counting on the Ross family to invite him there for the day. He had finished up with eating turkey and plum pudding with his landlady and the other elderly lodger, neither of whom had anywhere to go. It had been deadly, and he had had to pay his share towards the food and decorations.

'Mum had a bad chill take her just before Christmas, and you know what that's like, Andy. She's better now, but she didn't feel up to much, and the boys were all out. There was just Uncle Zacchary and Mum and me.'

'Well, never mind, kid, we'll go gay now, eh? And I know I don't have to worry about getting you home early this time because I asked, and you're let off the lead for once, my girl! Why is that?' he asked, with sudden suspicion.

Linda smiled. She wondered what he would say if her reply really quoted her mother: that he was expected to be one of the family soon! Somehow Linda couldn't see Andy taking on such a responsibility (even if he could afford to) unless there was something very big indeed in it for him.

'Oh, they're getting used to you, I expect, and they trust you,' she said lightly. 'But I warn you, if you let them down just once, it will be curtains for you, lad! They won't be as easy with you as I have been!'

'I know, honey! Here, let's pull up! Something to show you that will prove how much I am to be trusted – even by you,' and he stopped the car carefully in a layby to give her his Christmas gift. A nice, neat, but rather old-fashioned little gold brooch with a tiny diamond in it.

'Andy, you shouldn't have!' she said, touched and a little puzzled. She would have thought Andy's taste in any article he had bought, would be more modern, less quiet. She stifled the tiny doubt that he hadn't bought it, because that would raise other doubts as to how he had come by it. Instead, she said, 'I'm very pleased with it, Andy! Thank you!'

'Well, how about a kiss, then?' and he

brought out an absurdly small twig of mistletoe and held it above her head.

That made her giggle, and forget to protest about kissing. She was aware, too, of a certain curiosity about how she would feel if he kissed her this time. Last time had been the first kiss ever.

His kiss was hard and hungry, but it left her curiously flat. Her mouth felt bruised, but there had been no answering spark in her, and it bothered her.

'I'm – I'm afraid my gift isn't very original, Andy,' she stammered, glad of any excuse to prevent him from repeating the experiment with the mistletoe.

He took the package from her, and opened it. 'Fags! Just what I needed! A whole hundred – honey, you are a peach!' and he would have kissed her again, but she held him off laughing.

'The party, Andy! We'll never get there at this rate!'

'All right, but I'll say my thanks later,' he threatened.

He drove carefully tonight; it wasn't his car. And the hotel *was* large and sumptuous after all. Indeed, most of the guests to this particular party were in evening dress. Andy had only a dark lounge suit, and Linda had the dress on she had made herself; short, a rather nice blue, that would do duty for a Sunday dress and the local social engagements she might be called on to attend. She felt out of it.

Still, Andy had obviously done his best to stage something for Christmas, so she threw herself into being madly gay, and hid, with determination, the fact that she was well aware Andy knew very few people here, if any. They looked important, and ignored the two newcomers.

Andy was acutely miserable. He began to drink early on in the evening, and soon left Linda to take part in the Paul Jones.

Beneath her happy laughter and gaiety, Linda wasn't enjoying herself much. She danced with fat elderly men and thin ones, but very few young ones – they were all anchored with their own partners, until by sheer luck, one cheated and hastily hopped back in front of her when the music stopped. Her heart almost stopped at the same time. It was the man in the Underground train!

If possible, he looked even more impeccable and distinguished than usual, in his white tie and tails. And there was no mistaking his delight in finding her.

'Linda! Who'd have thought you'd be here!

I've been searching everywhere for you! Have you moved from your home address?'

'No! Do you know it, then?' she asked in surprise. She was beyond thinking straight, this was suddenly so exciting, and her heart was doing the queerest little leaps and bounds. It was one thing to be locked against him in a packed train of Christmas shoppers, but another thing to be dancing with him, and he was a wonderful dancer.

'Isn't it in Crackington? 34, Field Street?'

'Yes, that's right! How did you know?'

'Weren't you in that contest at Shenstone Bay?'

'Yes,' she admitted. 'But how–'

'Well, then!' he said, with a comical lift of his eyebrows, as if that were all the explanation needed. 'You're so full of Christmas good cheer, you can't think straight, you funny little thing! Never mind, I've caught up with you at last, and I don't intend to let you go this time! I've got so many things to say to you that I just don't know where to start, but first of all, what are you doing with yourself at the moment? Re the swimming?'

'Oh, that! I'm practising straight swimming, for various contests. My uncle's coaching me in the mornings before I go to work!'

'Good heavens!' He looked quite shocked.

'Nothing else? What happened to that agent you trusted so much and who must have been good to get you fifty pounds (I think you said) for The White Slipper show?'

She blushed and looked away. 'I made a mistake. I thought he said that, but it was only fifteen. Still, it was a nice little sum to get unexpectedly.'

He looked down at her very oddly indeed. 'Linda, you know, you're being wasted. You really must allow me to–' he began, in such a serious voice that she looked up at him in surprise.

Their glances locked, and she experienced the most queer feeling: as if she had known this man all her life, and that suddenly it didn't matter that she didn't know his name. Nothing mattered except that he had found her and was as pleased as she was about it.

The music stopped, and the blonde girl Linda had seen on the train, threaded her way quickly to his side and laid a hand on his arm. The way she did it was so pro-prietary that Linda found herself thinking that they might also have been married, that girl and the tall distinguished young man.

'Darling, how you do stray,' the blonde girl said laughing. 'Daddy's been looking for you everywhere. Come on, don't keep him waiting,' and she looked away to indicate where he was, without even letting her eyes alight on Linda for one moment. Linda felt she might well have been invisible.

It was a huge ballroom and the crowds threading their way back to their tables soon swallowed him up, his partner still talking to him and drawing him towards her father.

Andy was just behind Linda. 'Come on, old girl! Been looking for you everywhere! Come and have something to eat!' he said. He looked flushed and she knew he had been drinking.

The band struck up again, and Andy and Linda were caught up in the couples taking the floor again. Then press camera bulbs began to flash in different parts of the room.

'The big shots getting their ugly mugs into the newspapers,' Andy muttered.

But after they had had some food, he danced with her quite a lot, almost as if he didn't want to let her out of his sight, Linda found herself thinking.

When at last the time came for them to go, he hadn't introduced her to a single person, and she was tired out with the effort of doing every dance with him, from sedate waltzing to the very latest Pop craze.

'Had a good time, love?' he asked, as they got into the borrowed car, and took off before the main crowds began to leave.

Linda agreed that she had, but it wasn't entirely true. She wondered how it was that her friend of the Underground had allowed that girl to whisk him off like that. That imperious manner surely suggested a strong tie, but couldn't he have introduced her, told Linda what he had wanted to with that other girl there too? Or didn't the other girl want that?

Linda remembered only too well the way that girl had taken his arm when he had been talking to Linda on the train. Oh, well, perhaps they were married, or about to be, so what was the use of thinking about him any more, she told herself tiredly.

'We must do more of this,' Andy said, in an important voice. 'Next time I'll buy the tickets!' which rather spoilt it all.

'Don't worry, Andy. It's all right doing that sort of thing over Christmas, but I haven't got a lot of time for it ordinarily. You know that, but thanks for the thought.'

When they reached her home, he tried to kiss her goodnight, but Linda didn't want any more of it. She didn't want anyone's kisses if she couldn't have those of the one man who could make her heart race and bound like that! Certainly not Andy, who still seemed to be able to arouse distrust in her for very little reason.

What had gone wrong with this evening? What was the real truth behind it? What would her mother have said if a young man had taken her to that sort of party and left her for so long to make her own amusement?

'Where were you, all the first half of the evening, Andy?' she asked. Unwisely, perhaps, but she was tired and dispirited, and impatient with him.

'Talking to a chap about possibilities for you,' he said at once, rather glibly. She could have kicked herself for asking the question and giving him such a chance. But she couldn't leave it alone.

'Not Max Welman by any chance?' she asked lightly, a devil driving her to aggravate him, see how he reacted.

He jumped again, as he had that other time and made the car swerve. 'What did you say that for?' he shouted.

'Oh, I thought he might have been there – there were a good many fat elderly bald men with glasses!'

It took Andy a minute for that to sink in

and when it did, he laughed. A little too loudly and long. 'Silly kid, he wasn't there! If he had been, we wouldn't have stayed!'

'Why?' she asked heatedly.

After a significant silence, he said, 'Because you're my client and my girl, that's why!'

Oddly enough she felt comforted after that, and her doubts about him fled away. She said goodnight and thanked him for the evening, and slept soundly that night.

Next morning, she was first downstairs. Christmas was over, and now she must return to her swimming practice harder than ever, she thought, as she picked up the newspapers.

On the front page was a picture of a hotel party, and because it looked familiar, she stopped in her tracks to read it. With a shock she recognised the party she herself had been to last night, and *he* was in it. That tall young man with the silver touching his hair; the blonde girl with her hand on his arm, and a white-haired man with his arm round her shoulders. 'Caroline Chadwick, with father and fiancé Max Welman, at the Silver Horse Charity Ball at St Edna's Hotel last night. Max Welman, the well-known pro- moter, is...'

The words danced before Linda's eyes,

and it was some seconds before the real truth hit her, and she tied up with the times she had met that young man and the things Andy had done and said. So *he* was Max Welman!

Chapter 9

Andy, of course, expressed surprise that she didn't know. 'You only had to ask me about the fellow!' he said, unblushingly. 'I don't see why you're so interested in him. You know he upset your mother and that she wouldn't have anything to do with him!'

It was the following Sunday and he had been invited to tea. Because the little house seemed rather full of people – Tom's Tess included – Linda and Andy had gone for a walk, and it was ironical that this crisis between them should take place at the same field gate where he had made her feel so small and provincial on that other occasion. This time, however, was just that much different: they had come to one of those crises and Andy refused to see it.

'You let me think that he was bald and elderly and wore glasses!' Linda accused him.

'If you jumped to that conclusion you only had yourself to blame, honey!' he said, trying to laugh it off.

'It won't do, Andy! Don't you see, I've said repeatedly, be honest with me.'

'And I am honest – I've said I'd tell you everything about what I'm doing in your interests, now haven't I?'

'But this is the most dishonest thing you've done yet!'

'*What* is? What's all the flap about, Linda? You've seen his name under a picture and just because you didn't happen to meet him at that party–'

'Oh, but I did!' she broke in. 'I even danced with him, if you must know! But thanks to you, I didn't know he was Max Welman, and I believe you deliberately let me think Max Welman looked like some fat elderly man so that I wouldn't know him if I did meet him!'

'You want to meet him,' Andy said slowly. 'You want him to handle your affairs. That's it, isn't it? You'd run out on me at the drop of a hat, if Welman asked you to let him handle your career! That's it, isn't it – in spite of all your fine talk about wanting someone like me to get you up the ladder, eh?'

He looked ugly, she saw it with surprise. A small-time agent, fighting for his very life, and he didn't care whom he trampled in the process.

'Yes, if he proved to be honest,' Linda said

steadily. 'And you haven't proved that, not ever.'

'Honest! Honest! That's all I hear from you! But have you been honest with me? You didn't tell me you'd danced with him!'

'I didn't know it was him! If you must know, I met him on the train in London. And he was the man in the lift at The White Slipper (only I didn't know that then!) and I do believe you knew he was there, and that was why – yes, you said Max Welman was there, and that was why you had hurried me away!'

'All right,' he said at last. 'So now you know. And I'd do it again and again, because I don't believe he'd be any good for you!'

'But you might let me make up my own mind!'

'How can you? You're only seventeen and you've lived a sheltered life. Besides, you know what your mother feels about it. Just mention Max Welman to her and see what she'll say!'

'I don't care, Andy. It's the way you've made me feel about you, that's upset me most! I'll never be able to trust you again, never! You see, that panto wasn't really a promise, it was just a bribe to let you use my name to get your old job back. The panto fell through – I think I knew it would! Well, these things don't matter so much now but one day they will, and it's no use, Andy. We'll have to split up. I don't want you to look after my interests, now or ever.'

'Well, you're going to!' he said, taking her by the shoulders in a grip that hurt. 'You're going to be a topliner, and I spotted you and you're mine. You're not going to ditch me, my girl, don't you think it, just because you've been dazzled by a glimpse of Max Welman. You wouldn't do any good with him, anyway, because that girl of his wouldn't have you within miles of him. She's like that! She keeps all pretty girls away from him. Know why? Because hc can't resist 'em. He's all charm and promises – they all are. But me, I need you, and I'd stick by you because I need you.'

'No, Andy, no, no! I don't want you!'

'Maybe you don't, but you're stuck with me, Linda. And don't you try to break away, because I've got a weapon. Your mother.'

'Andy, you wouldn't upset her!'

'Oh, wouldn't I? I'd make such a row and such an upset that what Welman did to her would look like the puny attempts of a child to cause an upset. And I can, too. I can tell her of things you got up to in London, without your brother knowing, that'd raise your hair off your head. Never mind about a chance meeting on a train – I can do better than that! And your mother would be so upset, you'd never hear the last of it.'

'And you think I'd want you after that?' she cried, aghast.

'I know there's no hope for me, that way,' he said calmly, 'but it isn't you personally I want. It's your career – me handling it. I'm determined. You can't stop me. And don't think you can trick me, Linda. I'm desperate. I've touched rock bottom – I can't go any lower. When you saw me in Trafalgar Square, I was almost out of my mind. I'd just been turned down by the last agent I could think of – there wasn't any other firm I could try. It was a mouldy clerk's job or the dole – and no work or roof over my head over Christmas. So just you remember that, my girl, and take on the fixtures I get for you without argument. You and I are going to stick together and go right to the top … or else.'

Max Welman went to the States the following week, on business that kept him on that side of the Atlantic for eighteen months. Film promoting, and among them his eternal search for a beautiful girl swimmer, with acting ability and charm. His last attempt at contacting the family of Linda Ross had met with a sharp rebuff. Her brother Tom had answered the door, and – primed already by the vigilant Andy – he wouldn't even listen to what the man in the super chauffeur driven car had to say. While not being exactly rude, Tom sharply informed Max Welman that his sister's career was already in someone's hands, and that was the last the Ross family wanted to hear about it.

Nonetheless, Max Welman kept tabs on Linda. She had caught his imagination. He cursed himself for not being quicker off the mark each of those times he had met her, but goodness knew there hadn't been much opportunity, what with noisy moving crowds and the constant vigilance of Caroline, who had also come with him on his tour of America. Caroline didn't let anyone get near him.

If it weren't for her father, Max told himself grimly, he would let Caroline know, in no uncertain terms, what he felt about her. But he knew how much longer her father had to live, and he didn't want a row. Caroline would upset her father on the least excuse, he knew, if it meant getting her own way. So, for the rest of that good old chap's life, Max was determined that there should be domestic peace, even if it was all sorts of a nuisance to himself.

His cuttings book which he kept on Linda's activities was one of the things Caroline didn't know about. It was supplied by agencies in England, and through the snippings they sent him, he watched Linda's rise in the swimming world.

Pictures of her, holding the Cup she won that first Spring he was out of England, a sad little smile on her face; the Brewery Shield, successive cups and medals in County activities, and then National events.

Side by side with these successes, throughout that year, came snippings of Linda that summer, doing stunts in a tank in a fairground. This made him angry, and was the cause of his contacting an old friend who was also a private enquiry agent. Max wanted to know who was pushing Linda into that sort of activity, and learned it was the man she had talked to him about – Andy Blane, the beginner agent.

In the Autumn Max learned she had left her regular job in the sports equipment shop cash-desk, and had been successfully auditioned for pantomime; a diving stunt in the finale, into a transparent tank specially arranged in the auditorium. A dangerous job, but one which she had apparently cheerfully undertaken. She smiled broadly from the photograph, in a glittering costume, Andy Blane with her.

After the pantomime season, Linda went back to straight swimming and worked very hard indeed, training with her uncle for the big international events. 'All I want is to please my mother and make her ambitions for me come true!' the caption beneath Linda's picture read.

It didn't sound like Linda, Max thought. Where was that gay charming happy child he had first seen on television, so long ago at Shenstone Bay? She must be rising nineteen now, at the height of her Olympics career.

He had an aching inside him to see her again, talk to her. He was sure that if he could only get long enough by her side, he would be able to find out, at least, if she was really contented with that slimy little eel Blane looking after her interests.

Andy dressed over-smartly now. It was easy to trace his rise in fortune, from the appearance behind her, in all the photographs nowadays. There was never an appearance of Linda, without Andy Blane was pushing in somewhere, and he looked a smart little

Mick, if ever there was one!

Max Welman was all set to return to England, the year Linda was nineteen. He had now floated a new company, a larger than ever affair that made him incredibly rich and much sought after. Caroline was worrying away at the subject of their marriage.

'Max, darling, why are you waiting? You know how much Daddy wants it.'

He looked sharply at her. 'Has he said anything about it?'

She shrugged and looked away. Outside the open window of Max's sitting-room, the golden landscape of California basked in the sunshine, but Max was mentally following Linda Ross in a jet plane to Scandinavia, where she was soon to enter the International Championships.

'You know Daddy, Max. He doesn't say what he wants. He just looks wistful. It tears at me. You know he told us how happy he was when we got engaged.'

'I know that! It made him happy,' Max agreed, firmly, rising to his feet. 'And that, my dear, is all I'm prepared to do for the moment.'

'But why? Why? He's wondering why we're waiting so long! You know he's always saying how he'd love to see his grandchildren start coming along!'

'All men your father's age say that some time or another. It's a sentimental streak in them that's good. A man of that age becomes hard if he hasn't any sentiment in him. But that's all it is. You and I know that you'd have fun as my wife but also that there's nothing in the world you'd shy away from more, than to start a family. Admit it, Caro!'

'Oh, Max, you make me so furious! You're always trying to make out that I'm hard and money-grabbing and all that! How do you know I wouldn't like children of my own?'

'I know because I watch you when other people's children are around. You can't stand the clean and tidy ones but you frankly lift your skirts aside when the sticky ones appear, and as to the noisy, naughty ones – well, you just fade out of the picture, and (let's face it!) you see to it that I go with you!'

'Well, you're my escort – I'm engaged to you! Of course you're supposed to accompany me when I leave someone's house,' she protested, surprised and hurt, and angry underneath. 'Anyway, be honest – you don't like young children any more than I do!'

He didn't contradict her. To do so would be to give away yet another secret, and time had taught him that to give away secrets to Caroline was to lose the beauty of them, too. To let her know, for instance, that his dream was to have a home and young children of his own, would be to give her yet another facet of his character to throw back in his teeth when she was in a temper, or to tease him about, either in private or in front of other people. No personal secret was safe from Caroline's sharp tongue.

'Darling, you're just being trying,' she wheedled. 'Let me tell Daddy we'll get married soon! I know it would make him happy!'

'I'm not sure that it would, and I'm not giving you my permission to say any such thing, Caro. For one thing, I feel it might worry him rather than please him. And for another thing, there isn't time to indulge in the luxury of a big white wedding before I return to Europe.'

'Return to Europe? I don't want to go!' she stormed. 'You didn't say anything about this before! Besides, I'm having fun here and the weather's foul on the other side of the Atlantic.'

'Caro, honey, I didn't say you were coming with me. You are staying here with your father.'

'Oh, no! Where you go, I go, too, Max!'

Caroline said decisively. 'Daddy's all right here. He loves it.'

Max looked consideringly at her. He didn't want her with him. He wanted a secret trip to Europe, to make one more attempt to contact Linda Ross. He thought of nothing else, no one else, these days. Newspaper reports were hinting that she was about to become engaged to that Andy Blane. He wanted to satisfy himself that if this were true, it either wasn't her wish or that she just hadn't met anyone else and she didn't really care. He remembered the way her little face had lit up when she had met him on the train, and the way her eyes had been filled with sadness when Caro had snatched him away at the dance. He had seen her leaving that Christmas party, and she hadn't looked particularly happy with Blane.

He had to know. He must find out, Max told himself.

His work was almost finished here. Nothing he couldn't leave to his excellent personal secretary – Addison Young – or to Tim Ripley, the best manager and contact man he had ever had. But how to get out without having Caro under his feet was another matter.

161

But, he thought, standing there looking down at her, he might use her to keep this trip of his really secret. It would be the only way, he admitted ruefully to himself, even if he didn't much care for the method.

'I'm going to one of those nasty Northern towns, poppet. You won't like that, now will you?' he murmured.

'Northern towns! What, Birmingham and Manchester?'

He laughed. 'Those are nice clean cities, honey. No, I mean the streets where the mills are– I've had a tip that there's a girl who might answer my constant search. But it's got to be kept a secret.'

'Well, all right, a secret! And I'll come with you!' she insisted, taking his arm. 'And don't try to talk me out of it. I know the weather will be wet and cold – it always is. And I know I shan't like the locale. But at least I shall know what you're up to if I'm with you, won't I, Max, sweet?'

'Caro, you're a sport! I knew I could rely on you. Now, this is what we do. We tell the press that I'm going somewhere quite different – Austria, Switzerland, anywhere you like, and we'll creep on a plane to Shannon then hop over to the North of England. Now you must play your part, and act

162

casual, and I shall be muffled up to the ears, because I don't want it to leak out what I'm doing. I've lost discoveries like this before. Get me?'

'I get you!' Caroline was secretly triumphant that he had let her have her own way and go with him. She knew he hadn't wanted her to go.

Max found there was no opposition to his plans at all. They went beautifully smoothly. His secretary and Tim Ripley were in on it, and Caroline (as he had half expected her to, and had indeed banked on it!) let the Shannon trip out to the press. It was his secretary, who was as tall and thin as he himself, who went with Caroline; muffled to the ears, and wearing dark glasses, he sat quietly immersed in his business papers, successfully fooling everyone.

Caroline herself didn't discover that it wasn't Max beside her until the press met them on arrival. Having tipped off the Press to expect Max travelling incognito (as Max had guessed she would) she was furious.

But by then Max had gone by jet to Sweden, a little ahead of Linda Ross and Andy Blane. He was accompanied only by his friend the private enquiry agent, whose special job on this trip was to let Max know when Linda would be alone. It was vital to him that Blane shouldn't know that Max Welman was trying to contact Linda, until he had had a chance of talking privately with her.

It seemed an impossible job to get them apart. Andy dogged Linda's footsteps much the same as Caro did to Max. It was well after the Championships were over, and the competitors scattering, that Linda was located. She had returned with Andy to the hotel at Blechenberg, the agent reported.

She had changed into an evening dress, and was sitting at a table in the corner of the restaurant furthest from the orchestra; tired, but satisfied, having won her own three events, all that she had set out for. She was waiting for Andy to join her, but he had found the bar and was apparently unconcerned at leaving her alone.

Max went over to her table, bowed slightly, held the back of the chair facing her and murmured: 'May I, Linda?'

She was so surprised to see him that she almost knocked over the empty glass at her elbow. Her colour came and went, and she barely nodded permission for him to sit down with her.

They sat staring at each other for a full

minute. She had changed so much, he thought sadly. She was so poised, so sophisticated, so very beautiful, but her eyes were still steady, there was still that intense sincerity in her face that had stolen his heart all those months ago.

And at last, all he could think of was to say: 'Hello.'

Her lips curved into the old sweet smile. 'Hello,' she echoed.

She didn't ask what he was doing there. She accepted it that he popped up in unexpected places. She was just so glad to see him that she was near to tears.

'You've changed, Linda,' he said.

'We all change. You have, a little,' she told him.

'Older?' he smiled.

She nodded. 'A little. But still nice.' She looked round. 'Andy should be somewhere. I'd like you to meet him. Is your fiancée with you?'

His smile fled. 'No. She's in England,' he said, with tight lips. 'Don't let's talk about her. I want to talk about you. Such a long time ago I saw you on television, and heard you speak. You were what I was looking for. I've been blocked at contacting you, at every turn, either by circumstances or people. But

I still want you, Linda. Nothing's changed. I've got a great future for you. I know you're still under age. All I want to hear is what you personally think about it. I believe you've been around enough now, to make up your mind.'

'You still want me for what?' she murmured.

'For the star part in a big swimming spectacle film I've been waiting to put on. You've got everything. I can find brilliant swimmers, beautiful girls, girls with lovely voices, girls with charm, but I never seem to get one with the whole lot ... until I saw you!'

She laughed, briefly, mirthlessly. 'That's funny. Andy said that to me, that day, at Shenstone Bay. He told me a tale about having a rich father who was a promoter, but I didn't listen to that. Gradually he climbed down until he said he'd wanted to meet me personally. I didn't believe that either. Then he climbed down altogether and said he was just looking for someone to push up the ladder, and drag himself up too.' Her eyes were infinitely sad. 'And now you, of all people, come to me with a similar story.'

Chapter 10

He looked quietly angry. 'Except that I don't happen to be Andy Blane, but Max Welman, and anyone can check and find that my story is the plain unvarnished truth. You know, there were times in our brief acquaintance when I got the feeling that you didn't know who I was.'

She nodded. 'That's true. Right up to this time, in fact. I wish you weren't Max Welman, really.'

'Why, Linda?' There was an undertone in his voice that she didn't understand, and the anger had gone. He reached across and took her hand but she hardly noticed. 'Why?'

'I suppose it was a dream world I was living in. You just someone ordinary, unattached; me, just someone ordinary, without an Andy Blane to distort the truth at every step of the way.' She sighed. 'But you *are* Max Welman, and that's all there is to it!'

He let go of her hand. 'I suppose you wouldn't care to enlighten me as to how it was you never knew my name?'

She nodded again. There was no point in keeping it a secret. Andy was neglecting her shamefully, and every day she was catching him out in some new little lie or deception. But her mother liked him, and made things so difficult for Linda to get free of him.

'It all started when I returned home from Shenstone Bay,' she began.

He was easy to talk to. Tracing patterns on the table cloth with her fork, she told him about the girl who had called on them, and the story she had told of Max Welman's perfidy, not only to her but to other girls.

'You believed this?' Max asked, shocked.

'We didn't know you then. Didn't even know what you looked like. I didn't know who you were in the lift at The White Slipper,' she said, and told him calmly and briefly about what had happened with the car and the fallen tree.

'Even in the train, just before that Christmas, I didn't know who you were,' she said, remembering, and told him how she had again run into Andy in Trafalgar Square, and how he had wormed his way into her life again. 'He appeals to my mother. She wants to see me marry him. But you see, I'll never trust him again. Even when he told me about that girl, that Caroline Chadwick who

168

called on us–'

His head shot up. '*Caroline* called on you?'

'Yes! She was the girl who was responsible for putting us against you! My mother was ill for some time after that – but Andy told me, a long time afterwards, that it had been a put-up job by you, gambling on us being so eager to get me into the limelight that we'd be prepared to go in on any terms. Why? Wasn't that true? Don't you even know about her visit to our house that day?'

'No! I did not! Believe me, I didn't know anything about that visit of hers, or of what she did! I can't believe it!' He sat thinking. It wasn't in him to say anything against Caroline, either to Linda or anyone else, but to him, tying everything up, it was painfully clear what Caroline had been up to, and had succeeded only too well. She had wanted to make sure that Max never met Linda – she had never liked his interest in his girl discoveries, but Linda's lovely face on television that day had made Caroline act in a peculiar way for weeks. But to think Caroline had gone so far as to do such a thing – not only to Linda, but to him!

'Look, I've got so much to talk to you about, Linda – have you had your meal yet, by the way?'

169

'No. I'm waiting for Andy. He said he wouldn't be a minute. I don't know what's happened to him.'

'He's in the bar!' Max said shortly. 'I've a telephone call to make. Will you excuse me? Then I'll be back.'

He bowed slightly as he left her. With Max, punctilious manners to women were an ingrained habit. With Andy, the question of manners never arose: he could even stay in the bar all this time and leave her like this without a word.

Making up her mind, she left her things on the table, and went to find him. He was just leaving the bar, with some other people. He frowned as he saw her, but remembered in time to chase the frown away with his usual turned-on smile.

'Linda! Poor sweet, I forgot I left you at the table. Look, get a meal and amuse yourself for a bit while I see these people – I've just met them and there might be something big in it for us – for you, especially! I'll be back as soon as I can, so don't worry.'

'But, Andy, there's something I want to–' she began, intending to give him a chance to meet Max Welman.

Andy cut right across her words, his eyes straying to his new friends, who were impatiently awaiting him at the door. 'Linda, you look all in!' he said, quickly. 'It's been quite a day for you. Why don't you get a tray sent up to your room? Take it easy, turn in early? You really ought to, you know! You look dreadful!'

'Yes. Maybe I'd better do that,' she agreed quietly. 'And you take your time, Andy. Don't hurry back. I'll quite understand.'

He looked uncertainly at her, but his new friends were moving off. He pecked at her cheek. 'I knew you would, angel – get a good night's rest! See you in the morning!'

She went back to the restaurant. Max had returned to their table and was standing there, puzzled.

'I went to find Andy,' she said. She looked rather white. 'I won't wait dinner for him after all.'

'Did you find him?' Max asked, signalling the wine waiter. 'I think you need a little something quickly! What happened?'

'He's gone off with some new friends. I tried to tell him about you, but he wouldn't listen to anything I said. He wants me to turn in early while he discusses with them something that might be good for my future.'

'Do you think it's true?' Max asked frowning.

171

'No,' she said steadily. 'I don't, but even if it were, I don't think it would matter any more. I think it's time I used my own judgment, and if you'll have me, I'd like to put my career in your hands.'

It wasn't pleasant, explaining to Andy, the next day. He had a hangover, after a thick night with his new friends. If they had discussed Linda and her future at all, he couldn't remember a thing about it, and wouldn't have discussed it, but for the picture that had been taken of Linda and Max dancing together, the night before. The Swedish newspapers made quite a bit of it; Max was welcome in their country, as they were trying to woo him to make films there, and Linda had carried off the main prizes that day in the swimming field. An interesting couple, one paper said. Another went further, and pointed out what a handsome couple they made together. Andy risked making his bursting head worse by getting into a fury about it.

'How sly can you get, Linda? You pretended you were going up to bed, and actually invited me to clear out, knowing all the time that that snake-in-the-grass was waiting for you in the restaurant! And you tell *me* you can't trust me!'

'It doesn't matter any more, Andy, because you and I are through!' she said, very quietly. 'I'll return to England with you, because as it's all arranged, that way will be more tidy. But after we've returned, you and I part.'

'Oh, do we?' he said nastily. 'We'll see about that! What about all the fixtures I've got for you?'

'What fixtures, Andy? There's nothing for me to do now – no more shows or pantomimes. I've fulfilled all those. There's nothing left!'

He was almost purple in the face. 'Oh, isn't there? What about all your future swimming fixtures, then?'

'You've forgotten, Andy. They come automatically, to Uncle and to me. We started it, without your help. We've just let you handle them as a matter of form, but you haven't done a thing on your own in that direction.'

He would have kept on, but his head wouldn't let him, and Linda had had enough. 'I'm going, Andy. I'll pack and meet you downstairs. Don't forget the time the plane leaves.'

'Oh, no, you don't,' he said, barring her way. 'Let's understand this right now – you ditch me, and I'll work on your mother! I can and I will, and if you don't want to see her ill again–'

'I don't think you will, Andy. I don't think even you could be that mean!' Linda said.

Her heart was thumping, though, as she left his room. She was quite sure in her heart that he would go to any lengths to keep her from Max Welman.

Max had had to depart early that morning. They were to meet again in England. There was other business he had to attend to first.

She thought she knew what that business was, and in that, she was correct. She had never seen a man look so coldly angry as he had, when he had found out what that girl, that Caroline Chadwick, had done to them. Linda wondered who she was, how she was connected with him.

And then suddenly it all clicked into place and Linda recalled that the girl in the picture with him at that party had been called Caroline Chadwick. In all the rows she had had with Andy since then, about him misleading her about Max Welman, she had forgotten to connect that girl with the girl who had called at their house that day. She had been so preoccupied with Max himself that she hadn't given a thought to his fiancée beyond the fact that the girl was blonde, beautiful, and very possessive.

Her face scorched. She had actually told Max about what his own fiancée had done to her mother! No wonder he had looked angry! No wonder he had said that he couldn't believe it! That, of course, would be what he had gone off so early for – to have it out with Caroline, who was in England.

Well, from what she had seen of Caroline, that girl would make her story good, Linda thought. Max wouldn't want to take her up after that. And she had broken with Andy.

It was the briefest struggle, and it was over very quickly, and Linda, surprised and rather exhausted, faced the fact that she didn't care what happened to her and her swimming future. The only thing she cared about was that now she knew the truth about Max Welman, and she loved him, and that nothing else would be the same. He had spoiled her for other men, and he wouldn't even like her after this!

Max didn't relish what he had to do. Caroline would be very unpleasant, and if she found she couldn't talk him round to her way of thinking, she would go back to California and worry her poor old father about it.

Max was sorry for Joe Chadwick and hoped he would understand, but Max knew he couldn't go on like this. As with Linda, honesty rated very high with Max, and he had been aware for long enough that Caroline wasn't averse to twisting the truth if it suited her.

Caroline was in a white heat of rage when he at last arrived at the Chadwicks' London house.

It looked cold and unfriendly, everything covered with dust sheets, and only the old caretaker there. He was very cross at Caroline arriving so suddenly without letting him know well in advance that she was coming. There had been hard words between them, because for the moment Caroline had forgotten that the house was shut up until her father's return to England. And here was Max, looking like a thundercloud himself, paying off his taxi with an air of finality, as if what he had to say would take some time.

'So you've decided to come back!' she stormed, getting in first. 'You've got a nerve! Sending me to Shannon on a wild goose chase! Making a complete fool of me when I discovered it was your secretary I was travelling with behind those dark glasses! And then you go to Sweden with that girl!

Now talk yourself out of that one!'

Max went in without a word, to the shrouded drawing-room, and carefully put down his hat and stick and gloves before turning to her.

Then he said, in a terrible voice, 'Why did you go to the Ross home in Crackington with a pack of lies, two years ago, about having been taken up by me, and badly treated? Do you realise you not only cost me the chance to make that film I've always wanted to, but you made Linda Ross's mother very ill indeed with anxiety and shock?'

Caroline recoiled before this bombshell from Max. 'I don't know what you're talking about!' she said at last. 'I've never been to Crackington in my life – wherever that is!'

'Going to brazen it out, Caro? Then you won't refuse to go there with me and find out who did go, using your name, and making such havoc of a lot of people's lives, will you?'

'Don't try to wriggle out of the mess you're in, Max!' she said, recovering. 'I haven't finished with you yet! We're supposed to be engaged to be married, remember? And you keep putting off our wedding date! Now I've found out!' she finished triumphantly. 'Now I know why – and I've been on the telephone to my father about it, too!'

'*Now* what have you done, Caroline?' he asked, shocked. 'What is it you think you've discovered now?'

'This!' she said, picking up a brown paper parcel from one of the shrouded tables. 'A complete cuttings book about that girl! Pictures and clippings you've been collecting and keeping secret for two whole *years!* And you've been engaged to me all that time!'

His lips tightened. She didn't know how far she was going, in violating his private papers like this, nor of speaking of Linda Ross like this. He couldn't have said why it mattered so much that Caroline should have looked at those clippings and newspaper photographs of Linda. He only knew he felt dangerously near to shaking Caroline until that silly smile of jealous triumph could be moved from her face.

'Give the book to me,' he said quietly.

'No! I'm going to burn it up! You shan't have it!' she shouted. 'And I'm going to tell the story to the press! They'll love it! Film tycoon yearns in secret over little shop-girl from the provinces! Oh, it'll make a pretty story!'

He mastered his feelings with difficulty. 'I daresay it isn't the only collection of her

178

clippings in the world,' he said mildly, 'but it's hard on your father to have to see his daughter shown up in such a mean petty light. You can't hurt me, my sweet – there are too many people dependent on my business world to care what I do in private. But you? It'll make you look rather mean and jealous, won't it? People will say hard things about a woman scorned and all that!'

'They would,' she said, white-faced, 'that's if I weren't already engaged to you.'

'Caroline, you're not expecting me to marry you after this? After you've shown me you wouldn't mind wrecking my business empire I've built up, because of a petty jealous whim of yours? Oh, no, my dear. After this, I'm afraid we're through!'

'You're jilting me? You dare to jilt me?' she cried.

'No, jilt is a hard word. I merely recommend to you that we would be far wiser to think again over the suitability of both of us as marriage partners. Personally I don't think two people could make a greater mistake.'

'It's the same thing, isn't it? You try it, and I'll sue you for breach of promise!'

'I wouldn't advise it, Caro, if only for your father's sake.' He looked steadily at her. 'Be reasonable, my dear. You and I haven't really hit it off for such a long time now. I've put up with a good deal for your father's sake–'

'My father! A fat lot you care about him! He's liable to drop dead any minute–'

'No, that isn't true, Caro. Let's stick to the truth for heavens' sake. He's a sick man, but with care, and *peace,* he'll last for many years. But there's also the question of his finances.'

'He's rich – richer than you'll ever be! He'll break you! He will, and you know it, if you try and jilt me!'

'Caro, he isn't all that rich. He's kept the truth from you because he knew how much it meant to you to feel there was a lot of money behind you. While we were engaged, it didn't matter much. You would have had my money too. But now, Caro, think what it will mean to him to have a lawsuit on his hands. No, he couldn't do it. It would impoverish him and you, too.'

'Then don't do it! Don't jilt me, Max! It's simple!'

He shook his head. 'My dear, after today, I could no more go through with this, not even if the alternative was my losing everything. If I ever marry, it must be to someone who is for me, not against me. Someone I can trust.'

'Oh, very pretty! As if I didn't know what

all that meant! I knew it that day when we were watching television and I saw the silly look on your face when you sat blathering about that girl! That shop-girl, just because she could swim a bit and win a mouldy little cheque and talk about a present for her mother! You made me sick!'

'*Caroline!*'

'You think you can stop me now? After where you were last night? Dancing with her, and it's all over the front page of the papers here, too! The same silly look on your face! Do you think I'm going to let you get away with it? Everyone saying he's ditching Caro Chadwick for some little unknown with a simpering silly face? No, no, *no!*'

She threw herself on the couch, dropping the parcel that contained his precious cuttings, but neither of them noticed now. When Caroline had a storm of weeping, it shattered everyone within earshot. The old caretaker appeared at the door, took in the situation, and shot out again.

In times past, Max would have gathered Caroline up in his arms, and promised her the earth if only to try and stop that storm of weeping.

Not any more. Today he just stood there, looking down at her, stupefied, thinking over what she had said about himself and Linda.

Had he really looked like that, that first time he had seen Linda on television? Did he look like that whenever he spoke of her? Was it true, that he was in love with Linda?

He stooped and mechanically picked up the parcel from the floor, and walked slowly out. Hardly noticing where he was going or what he was doing, he picked up his hat, stick and gloves, left that chilly house, and automatically hailed a taxi; a taxi taking him out of Caroline's life.

Yes, it was true ... the truth hit him like a ball of fire, a blinding light. Yes, he was in love with Linda.

Chapter 11

Linda's home-coming was decidedly unhappy. The family forgot their pleasure in her achievements in Stockholm, in their fury at her having broken with Andy Blane in favour of Max Welman.

Even the important looking envelope from the offices of the Max Welman Films Inc. in which Max's second secretary said that Mr Welman wished to see Miss Ross as soon as he returned to England from New York, couldn't make Linda happy. An uneasy background was the worst possible thing for her kind of activity, and even her everyday practising with her uncle went all wrong.

'See here, Linda, lass, I don't understand what's behind all this,' he said, as they walked briskly back from the Baths, by custom of years. 'I didn't even know you'd met Welman!'

'It's no use trying to explain it all to Mum, Uncle, but I'd like you to know the whole story, if you'll just listen and not say anything until I've finished,' Linda said slowly, after giving thought to the matter. Her uncle could be as unco-operative and resentful as anyone, if he felt he was being kept out.

So she told him – in as brief and un-complicated a manner as possible – just what had been going on. And then she waited.

'I see,' he said slowly, at last. 'So what you're really trying to say is, you've got all you can out of me and straight swimming events, and now you want the big time, and your name in lights. Eh?'

'No, Uncle, no! That isn't it at all!' Linda protested. 'I don't want Andy Blane. I don't trust him. I don't even like him any more. At the best, I was only sorry for him, I think, though at the time I thought I might fall in love with him. He … he gets me that way. When he's down, I feel it's my fault, and I'd do anything to help him, but when he's up, he gets cocky and hurts me, then I don't want to see him any more.'

'Sounds like true love to me,' her uncle said. 'But you've let yourself get dazzled with this rich chap that we haven't even seen yet! That's the truth, isn't it?'

'He means an awful lot to me, uncle, more especially because I've only just found out that he's Max Welman. It wouldn't have made any difference if he'd been quite poor.'

'Only you knew all along that he wasn't poor,' her uncle put in shrewdly, 'even if you didn't know his name!'

'I can't expect you to understand, but I have told you everything, and maybe you can tell Mum sometime. She just won't listen to me. She thinks Andy's right for me, and she says I imagine he's being dishonest to me when all the time he's working round in his own queer way for my best interests.'

'Yes, well, I don't know about that. I've always said he's a smart Mick on the make, but between ourselves, lass, I'd rather you had him than this Welman. At least Andy's our kind. Ordinary people, that's us. And ordinary people understand each other, even if they're not being a hundred per cent above board. I'd rather that, than see you getting married above yourself and us left out in the cold.'

Linda sighed before this outlook. She felt she could never reach her uncle nowadays, and she didn't understand that she had moved away from him. She had no idea that her outlook had been broadened so much, not only by travel and by meeting all sorts and conditions of people, but by the very fact that she had had to kick her own way to the top. She had, after all, nothing to thank but her own efforts. Her uncle had trained her, given her the best advice he had had to give, but other girls had had that much from their trainers and still not made the grade.

In a very worried, and rather sad frame of mind, Linda found herself en route for London, to see Max on his return to England. One half of her wanted to dance on air, to think she was going to be with him, working with him, in some new exciting work connected with swimming, but this was overpowered by degrees, as the train drew nearer to her destination, and she began to see that this new life would take her further from her own family and friends. Did she want that? After all, love for Max was only on her side; he didn't know it, nor must he ever know it, because Max was engaged to that detestable Caroline Chadwick.

Max came forward to greet her, across the carpeted space between his desk and the door.

There was no mistaking his delight at the sight of her, but Linda put this down to his business plans for her.

'I do hope,' he said, after he had greeted her, 'that your being here today means that your family have given up their old objections to me?' He smiled slightly as he said it, but Linda was again reminded that she was very much under age, and even though that didn't weigh much with her, it might very well in Max's case, because of the contract he would want to draw up.

'They don't like it any more than they ever did, but they are not going to try and stop me,' she said quietly. 'Still, I wish they would try and see it from my point of view. Uncle knows very well that I'm at the top, so far as Olympics are concerned.'

'And you can't go much further. No, I appreciate that. Just what is their objection, do you think, Linda?'

'It's giving up Andy Blane. It's no use, I can't go on with him and I've told him so.'

He nodded. 'It's a pity. I've got such brilliant things ahead for you. This film I want to make, would be the fore-runner of a series – about five in all. I want to film in the South of France, the Greek Islands, the East – you know, the shores of the desert, palms and all that – and I had thought of making a swimming pool in the country of the Aztecs – South America. That would make a very colourful and unusual film indeed. I wish I could make your family see what an enjoyable life it's going to be for you, as well as a great deal of money.'

'I've never wanted big money, not for myself,' Linda said slowly. 'I used to dream of making a comfortable income, to help my mother, but now I'm not so sure I wouldn't just rather be me, in a shop in Crackington, if it meant that my family was going to be friends with me.'

'You could have the whole lot, if they realised how happy you were, surely?' Max probed. 'Are you sure we couldn't make a compromise, so that everyone would be pleased? It has been done before,' he finished, smiling broadly.

'How do you mean?'

'I was thinking that if we kept Blane in, to do the light organising, for you, and I did all the contracts for my side, everyone might be pleased, including your family!'

Linda stared. 'I think you're being very generous. But it wouldn't work. You couldn't work with Andy, you know you couldn't!'

'I haven't tried yet. I'm supposed to be good at handling people, so they say. How would it be with your family, if we could make my idea work?'

Linda shrugged. 'I don't know. I'd be able to tell better if you were to meet my mother. She looks on you as a sort of ogre at present.'

'Then we'll arrange that,' he told her.

Her life ahead, as Max outlined it, frankly dazzled Linda. After the sheer drudgery of her training, morning after morning, in the Baths at home, winter and summer alike, and the hurried trips to the towns where the events were being held, sandwiched between her work in the cash desk of the sports shop, this was just sheer glitter, she thought.

'To visit the glamorous places abroad that I've read about – oh, I'd give anything!' she breathed. 'You know, I didn't think I'd hear another word from you after you left me in Stockholm!'

'Why not?' Max asked sharply.

'Because ... well, because of that awful business about your fiancée. I didn't realise at the time that I was talking about *her!*'

'Would it have made any difference if you had, Linda?'

'Yes, I think so,' she said steadily. 'Honesty is one thing, but to deliberately embarrass someone, or to hurt them if they didn't know already that someone close to them could do such a thing–' She broke off, biting her lip. 'Has it made any difference to you both, knowing about it, I mean? As far as my family is concerned, it's all over and done with. I ought never to have told you about it.'

'As it happened, it made little difference,'

he said, with a deliberation that wasn't lost on her. 'We're through, anyway, but mainly because of another matter. So don't worry, Linda, and above all, don't reproach yourself. I think I knew a long time ago, that Caroline and I would never make a go of things. It's just the way things are!'

She nodded, and sensing he didn't want to say any more about it, she let the matter drop.

They arranged that he should visit them to get over the meeting with Mrs Ross. Linda secretly dreaded it.

Max, however, was understanding, rather clever the way he went about it. The magnificent car, which Linda had mentally seen half filling their little street, didn't arrive. Max came, instead, in a small but powerful open tourer, which promptly won the hearts of Linda's brothers. Max himself wore easy weekend clothes: corduroy slacks and a thick-knit sweater with a polo collar, and he looked very much like her brothers on holiday. Mrs Ross was enchanted with him until she heard his name.

'*You're* Mr Welman?' she asked, as if she couldn't believe her ears.

'Now, Mum,' Linda murmured, warningly, for she had obtained her mother's grudging promise not to show her animosity when Max Welman did descend on them.

'It's all right, Linda – it's just that I'm surprised that he should look so – well, I thought it was one of your new friends, duck! That Andy told me– Where *is* Andy, by the way?'

'Mum, you never invited him over today! You knew I had invited someone and you promised!' Linda broke in.

'I very much want to meet that young man,' Max said firmly. 'I've a proposition to make to him, and I'd very much like your advice on the subject, Mrs Ross.'

And soon, of course, he had Linda's mother eating out of his hand. Linda's uncle was rather a tougher nut to crack, but Max won him over, too, after he had gone with him, on foot, to scc the Baths where Linda had been trained, and to discuss the merits of various swimming baths in this country and abroad. Linda's uncle had been in the Army in Greece, and reluctantly admitted to still wanting to hear about the islands. Only Andy remained adamant: he wanted Linda in his own hands, not sharing her with Max.

After Max had gone that day, Linda found Andy moodily strumming on the piano in the front room. 'Why wouldn't you co-operate?' she asked him furiously. 'Do you realise that Max Welman didn't need your help? He could have pushed you right out in the cold! And you have the nerve to be rude to him!'

Andy grinned. 'You for myself or nothing, baby,' he said, aggravatingly. 'Your mother likes me, even if you don't!'

'Just what are you up to, Andy?'

'I'm not up to anything,' he said, in a hurt voice. 'I'm just not going to be taken on as a small-fry hanger-on in the Welman band-wagon, and if I want to visit your mother regularly, I'm not going to be pushed out by you or Max Welman, either!'

'Are you quarrelling with Andy, Linda?' Mrs Ross asked, coming in at that moment. 'I'm sure you've no call to.'

'I don't understand you, Mum! Max is suggesting that Andy should keep on as he is at present, handling my affairs – and he won't do it! He's being nasty about it!'

'He doesn't have to do it if he doesn't want to, now does he, dear? Don't let your new fortune go to your head, Linda!' her mother said. 'I reckon you've pushed Andy about enough, from what I can hear of it from one and another of you! A good many young fellas wouldn't take it – and neither will he, once you're married! You'd better be careful, dear – men don't forget in a hurry, even though Andy is the most gentle chap I've come across.'

Linda gaped at her mother. 'Hasn't uncle told you what I told him?'

'He said a lot of nasty things about Andy that I didn't believe,' her mother said composedly. 'Zacchary can believe them if he wants to, but that doesn't mean I have to. Now, what's this about you putting off your wedding to Andy?'

'Who said I'd put off the wedding?' Linda demanded, looking round at Andy, but he was sitting innocently studying his hands.

'Andy told me you wanted it put off indefinitely. I reckon that's trying the poor lad too far!' her mother said.

'Andy doesn't always tell the truth. I didn't say indefinitely,' Linda said heatedly. 'I said now and for good! I've broken my engagement with him and he knows it! I'm just being forced by everyone – even Max! – to keep seeing Andy, for one reason or another. If it weren't so, I'd be content for Andy to go right out of my life, and that's the truth!'

'Linda, dear, have you gone out of your mind?' her mother said. 'What nasty things to say in front of Andy too!'

'Mother, what are you playing at?' Linda stormed. 'Don't you understand? I'm through with Andy, so far as I'm personally concerned. If you and the family – Max even! – wants to keep on with him, that doesn't concern me!'

'But you can't keep on like that, dear, if Andy's going to be handling your affairs, now can you?'

'She has no intention of me doing any such thing, Mrs Ross,' Andy put in. 'You see, she's weighed it all up, and one way or another, Welman's the better bet. Floating in money, you see, and Linda knows I'll always be hard up.'

'Oh, Linda, how can you be so mercenary?' her mother cried.

Linda looked from one to the other of them. Andy was smiling faintly; he had achieved his object, driven her out into the open. Her mother had just been his pawn, saying everything he had hoped she would say.

'I'm not mercenary, Mother,' Linda said, in a low fierce voice. 'It just so happens that I'm in love with Max. I wouldn't care if he hadn't a bean – the whole thing is, I can trust him. I'd trust him with my life, and he's the only man I've ever felt like that about, or ever likely to – much good though it may do me!'

'Oh, dear, I feel quite faint!' Linda's mother said, sitting down suddenly. 'Oh, it's all these upsets! Why couldn't you stick to your straight swimming, with your uncle training you, and Andy going to marry you? I would have been so happy, Linda – and now look how you've messed it all up!' she said, starting to cry.

'I haven't messed anything up, Mother!' Linda sighed, getting up to get her mother some brandy, by long habit, when one of these scenes flared up. 'Max doesn't know I love him – I was forced into admitting it just now and I don't want you two to say any-thing to him, ever! It's private and personal. Anyway, he wouldn't care if he did know. I mean nothing to him. I'm just the new star he felt he wanted, when he saw me on television that day. He's said so, so don't worry.'

Her uncle came in quietly at that moment, a peculiar look on his face. 'I – er – Welman's come back for his cigarette case – that big black and gold one he had in the armchair. Oh, there it is – I'd best give it to him.'

'He's here?' Linda whispered.

Her uncle nodded and went out. He came back almost at once. 'That's queer. He's gone. I suppose he heard you all having a row in here and didn't want to embarrass anyone.'

'I didn't hear that noisy car of his!' Mrs Ross said, leaning forward.

'He left it at the top of the road, when he found out he'd left his cigarettes behind, and just walked back. Save turning it, I suppose. Oh, well, I suppose Linda can give it to him next time she sees him. But I do think it's a pity you can't keep your voices down when you don't agree,' her uncle finished, angrily. 'Me, I rather liked that chap!'

'Yes,' Andy said, getting up. 'That's how he wins everyone over. I might as well bow myself out, for even you, Mrs Ross, will be falling for the Welman charm before long. I can see it happening, and I don't think I'll stay to see my last ally turn against me.'

'No, Andy dear, don't go! I shan't ever turn against you!' Linda's mother cried. 'And I'll talk our Linda round soon, to your way of thinking! You'll see!'

Linda herself was less interested in Andy, than in whether Max had heard what they were talking about.

Tactfully, her uncle denied it. 'No, you

were all shouting about money and whether Andy was being treated right. Can't expect a chap to want to stay and hear all that, after he's laid himself out to make an offer to a man he doesn't really need. I reckon that Max Welman has done Andy proud, the way he treated him. I'd like to tell him so, too, only I don't want to upset your mother.'

Linda was persuaded that Max hadn't heard her say she was in love with him. By the time she had to go and see him again, the row was forgotten at home, and her mother was hopefully talking about Tom's engagement to Tess, and when they were going to be married.

'Tess would like to be in the pictures, Linda. Do you think you could speak to Mr Welman about her? She's such a nice girl.'

'We'll see, mother, later,' Linda said, carefully, to avoid upsetting her mother again. 'Meantime, I've got to get my own contracts signed.'

Max Welman's offices in London were inclined to intimidate Linda. She felt she would never get used to being passed from one to the other, from the doorman in his smart uniform, upwards through the ranks of all the officials until Max's private secretary escorted her the last stage of the journey in the private lift to his magnificent office at the top. By then Linda was certain that this was as unreal as it was at first, and that the film contracts would never be signed. There would be a snag somewhere. This was all too good to be true.

The minute she saw Max, she knew that this was going to be different from last time. The look in his face as he came to meet her, made her legs feel like jelly.

'Hello,' she said, speaking fast to hide her nervousness, and for the sake of something else to say quickly, she remembered the cigarette case she had to return to him and got it out of her handbag. 'You left this behind at our house. Did you miss it?'

'I did indeed, Linda,' he said, his voice deep with emotion. 'And I heard what you said. About me. Was it true? Did you mean it?'

He took her face in his hands, so that she couldn't turn away from him. She nodded speechlessly. She couldn't have spoken a word just then, her throat was too tight.

'Did you really mean it when you thought I had no more interest in you than as a star in my films?' he persisted.

'You had no right to stand and listen!' she burst out, tears spilling over her lids, her voice thick with emotion. 'How could you listen when you must have known you weren't intended to? Why didn't you go away?'

'My dear, I was too stunned to move! Your poor uncle was just as rooted to the spot as I was, till he pulled himself together and shot in to no doubt tell you all I was there. Didn't he tell you I heard it?'

'No. He said I was just talking about money and Andy.'

'Tactful man. But I'm so glad I did hear, my dear, for if I hadn't, I'd have gone on thinking that Blane had got you firmly twisted round his little finger, in spite of all you said to the contrary, and I'd have gone on loving you to the end, without saying a word.'

'Loving me?' Linda whispered, blinking fiercely.

'You didn't know?' he said, drawing her into his arms. 'You didn't know I loved you from the moment I saw you, on television? Oh, my dear, my dear!' and he kissed her, a long tender kiss that made his sumptuous office swim round her until everything was just a blur, and Max was the one solid thing in all the world to cling to.

Chapter 12

Filming began much sooner than Linda had expected, but she was no judge of time nowadays. Time slid by on golden wings, she thought, as she waited one day for Max to call for her in that sumptuous car of his.

The South of France had always been just a romantic name, to Linda. Now, standing at the tall window of her hotel bedroom, looking out into the hot sunshine that made the white of buildings and pavements hurt the eye, she reflected that she had never been so happy in her life before. She loved the tropical foliage, the bright hurting blue of sea and sky, but most of all she loved the swimming sequences in the film.

Although she had to do as she was told, yet the swimming wasn't in any way as arduous as it had been under her uncle's direction at the Crackington Public Baths. It was, too, sheer joy to move her body in the warm waters of the Mediterranean, when the filming was over. Sheer joy to have Max with her all the time, and to read the message of love and adoration in his eyes.

Her happiness was clouded, of course. Her family had been very angry when they had first heard that Max returned her love. Her mother had another 'turn' and prophesied that it was all glamour and that none of it would last. Tess was frankly jealous, and Linda's brothers protested that a life with such a smooth customer as Max Welman would only make Linda unhappy in the long run. And there was Andy...

Andy had said he was glad. He had turned right round and protested friendship, said she could rely on him to do everything he could for her. Andy's change of heart had made Linda more miserable than any of the others; Andy was unpredictable, but when he acted generously he was to be feared as much as anyone.

But that was all six months ago. Since then, Linda had been much photographed in the press and in the news, on television and film strip. She was so used to being photographed now, that it was as natural as breathing. As natural as being seen about with Max, in that wonderful car of his.

The only thing that nagged at her was that in spite of his love for her, his tenderness, his wonderful gifts and never-failing attention,

Max had never mentioned engagement or marriage to her.

A car pulled up outside the hotel. She couldn't see who was getting out of it, from her window, because the striped awning was in the way, but people passing by stopped to stare, and there was a good deal of attention from the uniformed doormen. Was this Max, as usual?

Linda caught sight of the flick of a girl's skirt, as she passed along beneath the awning. Linda's heart began to hammer for no reason at all. She hadn't seen Caroline Chadwick since the girl had been in the news at the time of Max's telling Linda he loved her. Caroline had left for California, where her father was said to be very ill. She had looked bowed down with grief, Linda remembered, in that photograph, and Linda herself had wondered if she had taken Max away from that girl at a time when she had needed him most. She had had to sharply remind herself that Caroline had served her own family a very dirty trick and made her mother really ill.

Standing at the window waiting for Max that day, Linda wondered where it would all end. She didn't even feel like that girl who had won the cheque for two hundred and fifty pounds at Shenstone Bay two years ago. She was now poised, sure of herself, a much publicised young lady with a lot of swimming trophies, apart from her connection with Max as his new star.

Linda remembered her Aunt Mary's manner when she had flown back to England for a lightning visit a few weeks ago.

'Where's my favourite niece gone?' Aunt Mary had said. 'I'm frightened of you, my dear – you look like the Ice Maiden in the fairy story.'

'That's only my make-up,' Linda had joked. 'I daren't laugh or it will all crack!' But her aunt hadn't laughed.

'Have I changed so much?' she asked herself, searching her face in the long gilt mirror over the ornate dressing-table. But to her, the reflection was still of an anxious girl, a girl who loved so deeply, but who still wasn't sure of her man.

The telephone bell rang. 'Mr Joe Chadwick has called to see you, Miss Ross – are you free?' reception enquired.

'Yes, of course – ask him to come up to my suite,' Linda said, but her heart was hammering fit to choke her.

What did the formidable Joe Chadwick want with her? Joe Chadwick, that girl's father – the man who had made Max, so legend had it, and could break him now, if he wanted to. Linda never questioned that last bit, or she would have learned that it was merely spread abroad by Caroline herself, and that it wasn't true.

She waited for him, her heart banging against her ribs, and she had the shock of her life when there was a tap on the door, and both doors were flung wide to push in an invalid chair, in which sat – not the huge, bombastic man she had expected and dreaded to meet since Caroline had gone out of Max's life – but a little frail old man with white hair and shiny pink face, and two of the most brilliant pale blue eyes she had ever seen.

'Oh, I'm sorry – I didn't know! I would have come down, not asked you to come up!' Linda gasped, going towards him.

'Don't worry, my dear! I hoped you'd ask me up to your suite, so that we could have a private talk,' he said, in a soft voice weakened with illness, and he dismissed his attendants. So this was what the flap downstairs had been, Linda thought, and wondered who the girl's frilly skirt had belonged to. Just another visitor, she supposed.

'Have you come all the way from California, ill like this?' Linda asked.

'Yes, but not entirely to have this talk with you,' he smiled. 'I had many reasons for coming. This was only one of them. I wanted also to see Max again. Max was like a son to me, you know.'

'Yes, I know. He often talks to me about you.'

'Does he, now? I thought perhaps he'd forgotten all about me. You see, my wife died before she could give me a son. Just my daughter. I've never married again, and when I thought Max was going to marry my daughter, and become my son-in-law, that, to me, was the next best thing.'

'And you think I robbed you of him?' Linda asked.

'The newspapers say you did,' he said quietly.

'I didn't, you know. I had no idea he'd broken with Caroline, and he assured me it was something quite different.'

'Different from what?' the old man asked quickly.

Linda twisted her hands together. 'I can't tell you that. It's something between Max and myself, and it doesn't really matter any longer. It concerned my mother, and she's quite well again.'

'I see. You know, my daughter's a very shy girl. There are some people who may think she's rather cool and aloof, but that is her greatest handicap. An inability to make friends or to win people's confidence. Max is the only one who has ever understood her, the only man likely to make her a good husband. I've watched them, many times, and felt that they were ideally suited to each other.' He sighed.

'Things have changed, Mr Chadwick,' Linda urged.

'My dear,' the old man said, with his kind, wise, sweet smile, 'in the course of a long life I have come to admit to myself in all honesty that things don't change of their own volition. It's people who change things.'

She frowned slightly. 'What are you trying to say to me, Mr Chadwick?'

'Don't think I'm giving you a lecture, my dear. I'm just trying to let you see into my mind. I'll be frank: I myself have been guilty perhaps of trying to change things to suit my own convenience, all through my life. And that is what we have to ask ourselves: who is going to benefit? Ourselves – or other people? Now, when Max was all set up to marry my daughter, it was going to benefit her, himself (make no mistake about it, he

206

knew her from childhood and they understood each other, and I was like a father to
him!) and also it would have benefited me.
I'll admit it. I always wanted it. But now
more than ever.'

He paused, with tremendous effect. 'You
see, I haven't much longer on this earth. I
would die happy if I were to see my daughter and Max settled in life together. So you
see my point: if Max and you – by the way,
are you engaged yet?'

Linda shook her head.

'What does Max say about it? Does he
want to marry you soon, or when this film is
finished?'

'He hasn't mentioned it yet,' Linda was
forced to admit. 'He has told me he loves
me and I love him.'

His face cleared. 'Oh, I see! Then perhaps
I need not have troubled to make this journey or to incommode you with embarrassing questions. Forgive me, my dear!'

'Just a minute, Mr Chadwick! You can't go
without explaining what that means!' Linda
said sharply. 'Are you saying that Max
doesn't want to marry me?'

He spread his hands and shrugged. 'Who
knows? I can only say I am vastly relieved to
hear that this is just a repetition of an old

pattern, so *far*. You see, most of these film magnates have so much to lose, and Max himself by his very charm is inclined to use his own methods to keep his newest star happy. It stands to reason, all those vast sums of money sunk into the moods and abilities of one young lady. So he makes her feel happy and contented while she is working for him. Nothing wrong in that, is there?'

'You mean he's just playing me along, for his film? I don't believe it! Not Max!'

'Oh, come now, don't be like that about him! He's a very fine young man, and I'm sure he wouldn't dream of misleading you as to his intentions. If he says he loves you, then he loves you, but just remember: a man like Max can love many people at the same time. He's a remarkable young man!'

Linda was stunned. She watched him slickly turn his invalid chair and when he was near the door he rapped on it with the tip of his stick. His attendants appeared and in no time at all he was gone. A gentle, sweet old autocrat. She must stop him. Find out what he intended to do. She couldn't just let him come into her life like this, without warning, and snatch away every scrap of happiness

208

she had.

She ran down the corridor, but the lift was disappearing. She rang for the second lift, but it was so long in coming up that she took the stairs, in desperation.

Joe Chadwick was being pushed out to his car when she at last reached the bottom. A huge car, with a specially constructed back to wheel the chair up into. With him was that girl, the blonde who had been on the train with Max. Linda had no trouble at all in recognising her; hers was the frilly skirt that had flicked into view under the awning. Where had she been while her father was talking to Linda?

Before Linda's stunned gaze Andy's figure flashed into view, bending over the girl as she shut the car door. Then stepping back, he sketched a salute with his right hand, and turned away, smiling in that self-satisfied way that Linda knew so well.

'Andy!' she called, going towards him. 'What are you doing here?' she asked sharply.

'Linda! I was just on my way up to see you,' he said, but the statement was too glib. She could tell, after all this time, when he was lying.

'Don't bother to come up. We can talk down here,' she said, leading the way to chairs on the terrace. 'What were you doing with that girl and her father?'

'Welman's fiancée happens to be a friend of mine,' Andy said calmly.

'She isn't his fiancée any more!' Linda gasped. 'That's all off – ages ago. Max told me so!'

'Did he?' Andy said, indifferently.

'Yes, he did! And it's true!'

'All right, if that's what you think, okay. Now, what did you want me for, Linda, because I do have things to do, you know!'

'Am I going mad? What's making those two, that girl and her father and now you, think she's still engaged to Max? What made Mr Chadwick come all the way from California, and why didn't he see Max at the same time?'

'Search me,' Andy said, getting up. 'Look, I'll have to go, if that's all you've got to say.'

'It isn't all I've got to say, Andy Blane, so don't pretend to be all calm and collected with me,' she said, her temper rising. 'You're up to something! I can recognise all the signs. There isn't any reason for those two people to be so cordial with you, if you aren't in on something with them!'

'I wouldn't say those things, if I were you,' Andy commented. 'If you must get all heated about it, do it with your pal Max. And ask him, at the same time, what all this is about a Breach of Promise case being dangerous to old Joe's dodgy health. That might explain why your Max isn't publicly announcing his great love for his newest star. Think about it, honey!'

Linda couldn't believe it. She went back to her suite to think it all over, and her head reeled. Her bewilderment had the effect of staving off what would have been a very great grief, for Max's attitude had been gently nagging at her for long enough, and this looked as if it were the real reason behind it all. But why couldn't Max have told her, if he were still considering Joe Chadwick above the girl he was supposed to love so dearly?

She resolved to have it out with Max when he called for her, but that day he broke the pattern. He sent his chauffeur-driven car for her, and when she did see Max, she had no opportunity to speak to him alone.

For days she fumed and fretted because she couldn't see him alone. In the evenings, instead of dining alone with Linda, either other film bigwigs, or close friends of Max's, dined with them, and one night he asked her to excuse him altogether, as there were people he had to see.

'The Chadwicks!' she told herself, her throat going tight. 'Who else?' And sitting there alone in her sumptuous apartment, Linda experienced the first prickings of defeat. That girl, Caroline Chadwick, was working to get Max back again, and she had roped Andy in to help her, Linda told herself, shaking all over. Andy with a chip on his shoulder was a formidable enemy. Caroline, having lost Max to Linda, would, she had known all along, be unforgiving. And Caroline didn't use clean methods with which to fight. How could Linda hope to succeed against such overwhelming odds, to keep Max?

What hurt most of all was that Max never mentioned Caroline and her father, in spite of their coming to the South of France.

Unable to bear it any longer, Linda taxed him with it one day. 'Aren't you going to tell me what happened, Max?'

He stared. 'What happened about what, my sweet?'

They were resting between sequences: a rare moment of being alone together. Linda's skin, a beautiful even tan, glistened in the sunshine; her hair fitted her like a tight black cap with the new styling, and her lips and eyebrows had been altered, too. But her eyes were the same; serious, worried even. Max leaned forward.

'Is anything wrong, Linda dear?'

Her heart hammered painfully. How could he sound as if he knew nothing about it, when that nice old man had been so vehement about it? 'The Chadwicks – Caroline and her father. Have you been seeing them?'

'What *do* you mean, Linda?' Max sounded irritable now. The swimming sequences hadn't gone so well lately. She knew it. She was too worried and unhappy to do well, and she was haunted by what her uncle had said once; when a swimmer reached the top of the ladder, it was so easy to slip back, a long way back. Was she slipping back?

She opened her mouth to say that they were in the South of France, when it occurred to her that it wouldn't be possible for him not to know that. They were so much in the public eye. And how could she say that Caroline's father had been to see her and tell her that Max didn't really want to marry her, but was just playing her along for the sake of the film? If it were true, it would be so embarrassing for both of them, and betray her anxiety about his not proposing to her. If it weren't true, it would make her appear to doubt Max. Either way, it would look ghastly, she told herself.

'Don't be cross with me, Max,' she murmured, so that the others moving around them wouldn't hear. 'I thought the Chadwicks were here in the South of France, that's all.'

He bit his lip. 'Caroline is, but I hardly thought you'd be interested. She contacted me about her father. He's in England, and not too good.'

So Mr Chadwick hadn't been to see Max while he was here! Now she didn't know what to say, because Max had evidently seen Caroline – how many times she had no idea – but he hadn't meant to mention it to Linda, that was clear!

The serenity between them evaporated after that episode almost as if Caroline's influence had found a chink and was widening it into a gulf, forcing Max and Linda apart.

Andy came to see Linda one night. 'Look, I'm sorry I was a bit tetchy that day, when the Chadwicks were here. You caught me out, rather. I mean, I didn't want you to see me with them, in case you thought I was running out on you. I know they're no friends of yours.'

214

'They told you about what was discussed that day!'

'No! I meant I knew you'd never forgiven her for upsetting your mother that day,' Andy said swiftly; too swiftly. 'Look, you know I'm supposed to be acting for you, for the small stuff. Would you do an odd job for me, Linda? Wait – the fact is, I'm hard up, and rather than ask you to lend me the cash, I'd prefer it if I could fix up a job for you on the side, so I could get the commission. What do you say?'

'All right, if it's okay with Max!'

'I don't have to ask him about the small stuff, Linda! He wouldn't thank me for bothering him, anyway. Besides, this is just a small advertisement for T.V – Linda Ross, the famous swimming star and gold-medallist, always uses Quinn's Certain-sure Rubber Caps and Shoes. "I wouldn't feel safe without them." Get the idea? Then you dive into a little pool and swim a bit – sixty-five seconds and wait till you hear how much! And how can Max object to that?'

'I'd rather contact him first, Andy,' Linda said.

'Okay. Go ahead!' Andy said, shrugging, and helped himself to a drink while she asked for Max's number.

He couldn't contain himself while she made her call and put the receiver down. 'Not in, Linda, love? Bad luck!'

'Not in!' she said between her teeth. 'He's flown to England – with that Caroline Chadwick! And he didn't even tell me! I had no idea!'

Andy mastered his triumph with difficulty. 'Not to worry – it might have been done in a hurry. Well, look, you can please yourself about this now, love, can't you? You did try to get him on the blower – and a chance like this won't wait!'

'All right,' Linda said. 'I'll do it!'

The more she thought about it, the less important that little ad seemed to be. Just a quick whisk into the studio, a brief rehearsal, and then it was over. A rush job, expertly wedged in between the star's work on Max's film, by Andy and the photographer.

Max's producer was carrying on with the shots that had already been rehearsed on the film, until Max returned. It should have gone easily, but it didn't. Linda couldn't do anything right while she was in this state of mind. It appeared that everyone knew about Max's sudden departure except Linda.

'Well,' the producer tried to reason with him, 'it was to be expected, wasn't it, Linda?'

216

'What was?' she asked blankly.

'The old boy's heart has always been dicky, and it was natural for Max to go back to England with her when they heard of this new attack of her father's! After all, Max and Caroline – well! – they have always been– Oh, lor, am I being frightfully tactless?'

So that was what it was! Linda went off by herself, to think it over but, passing a newspaper lying on a chair, she found Max staring up at her from its front page. Standing on the top of the airliner steps, his arm round Caroline's shoulders, helping her down; Caroline crumpled with grief, looking up to Max for sympathy and support. 'Max Welman takes time off from filming in the South of France to rush to Joe Chadwick's bedside with Caroline.' And beneath, the caption asked the simple question: *Together Again?*

Chapter 13

Everything seemed to blow up in Linda's face on Max's return. He came alone, and was clearly not in a good temper.

Word got around the whole company, in the way that had always mystified Linda, that Max was having high words with his producer, about the lack of progress in his absence; there had been trouble over the 'rush shots', and over the time and money wasted when all had been arranged quite clearly and simply. (Max was no better than the next man, when it came to taking money losses.) Then he heard about the advertisement which Linda had done, and that, it appeared, was the end. Max sent for her.

'What,' he asked, in a dangerously quiet voice, 'is the meaning of this contract, Linda? This advertisement film for Quinn's while you were working with me?'

'Why don't you ask Andy?' she retorted. 'I'm only the star, who does as she's told!'

'What is that supposed to mean?' he asked icily.

'Andy came to me and told me it would be all right and that you'd given him permission to do as he liked. I did try to speak to you on the telephone about it, but I heard that you'd gone off to England with Caroline Chadwick, without even mentioning it to me! Thoughtless, wasn't it, Max? At the very least, not very polite!'

'Oh, so that's it! My fool of a secretary forgot to tell you, so this is the way you show off your temper! I've seen that temper of yours before, Linda, but you didn't have to take it out on me like this, did you?'

'I must be going mad!' she breathed. 'What have I done? I can't work for two masters! It was your idea that Andy managed the smaller things for me – not mine! I wanted to work only with you, but oh no, you had to have Andy Blane in. Well, don't blame me if he fixes something for me to do, which you don't happen to like! I'm only the pawn, the poor simpleton who swims – and it seems I can't even do that to please everyone!'

'Don't shout at me, Linda!' he said, and if she had been cool enough to notice, she would have realised that Max's temper, like that of most people who are slow to anger, was very intense when it was aroused. 'I agree that your swimming sequences haven't been

219

all that I had expected of you. Perhaps you're working too hard? Perhaps we all are! Well, I suggest that you go back to England for a rest. I can do some other scenes meantime. Perhaps we can all cool down by then. But please, meantime, don't do anything else like the Quinn advertisement. I shall have to get my lawyers to straighten this one out. I see it's no use trying to explain to you what it's all about while you're in this mood – all I would say is, don't do it again!'

'Why don't you tell Andy Blane that?' she flared.

'I'll see him next,' Max promised, more quietly this time. 'That's all for the moment, Linda.'

She stared, unbelieving. 'Is that *all* you have to say to me, Max? *All?*'

'Yes, if we don't want to quarrel openly,' he said, not looking at her. 'I've only just managed to avoid one lawsuit and now I come back to France to find you've almost involved me in another! What more do you want me to say?'

He reached for the telephone then, and she realised he had dismissed her.

Blinded by tears, she went back to her own suite, and cried heartbrokenly. Then she remembered Andy.

He was there, when she called him up, and apparently quite unperturbed. 'Sweetie, I didn't make you do the ad – you wanted to do it! You know you did! You were so hopping mad to find Max had gone back to England with Caroline! Now isn't that so?'

'But you came to me about the ad in the first place!'

'No, love, I came to tell you about Max – to save his secretary who was rushed off his feet – but I couldn't get a word in edgeways, and before I realised it, you were phoning Max, and found out for yourself that he'd gone to England!'

'Andy, you're twisting the truth, as usual!'

'Don't shout, darling, or the phone will go up in smoke! Well, all I can say is, it's your word against mine! I ask you, would I be the one to suggest you did an ad for Quinn's? Would I, considering Max is tied up hand and foot with ads for Quinn's rivals? Holy smoke, what have you done?' and Andy started to laugh, softly, before he put down the phone.

Not finished yet, Linda called Max up on the telephone. 'Max, I didn't know about Quinn's being the rival firm! I didn't, honestly I didn't! I don't know much about how these business deals are worked, or I wouldn't have done it! But Andy said–'

'Linda,' Max broke in, 'I know you don't like Blane and didn't want anything to do with him, and didn't like it because I wanted to give him a chance, but if you had to discredit him, did you have to do it in such a big way that I can't ignore it? He hasn't got a bean, so how can I chase him for this? In hitting out at him, you're hitting me! Do you realise it?'

'I haven't done a thing to Andy,' Linda said desperately. 'It was all his idea. I've just been on the telephone to him and he's pretending it was all my idea but it wasn't! It wasn't!'

'Why didn't you wait till I came back? You knew I wasn't going to be away long!'

'I didn't! I didn't know anything about it, and the producer said–'

'Now please, Linda, don't try and involve anyone else, in your efforts to get out of it. You were in a hurry to do that ad, now weren't you? It was literally a rushed job!'

'The man at the studio wanted to rush it!' she cried.

'Now you're pulling him in.'

'Do you mean you don't believe anything I say?'

'I don't know, Linda. I don't know how

much I can believe you about anything. Why didn't you tell me Caroline's father had been to see you? That poor old man, going all that way, in his state of health–'

'Max, it wasn't my idea! It was his!' Linda protested.

'All right, so it was his idea. Are you going to tell me what happened, when he went all the way up to your suite in that invalid chair of his?'

Something snapped in her. 'No, I don't think so. I don't understand what's got into you, Max, unless what he said was really so. In that case, I apologise for thinking I meant anything more to you than any other girl you might take up. And if you can find another swimmer to take my place, I wish you'd do so. I'm going home.'

There was a plane due out in half an hour. Under happier circumstances, Linda thought wryly, there would be no plane for hours, but because she was leaving part of her heart here, Fate was unkindly making the way easy for her to be hustled away from the sunshine and the warmth and the man she loved, back to England.

An England grey with lowering skies and seas; a sultry England threatening a storm.

The airport looked about as unwelcoming as a desert. Linda couldn't face a chilly reception at her home, so instead she decided to go to the coast, to visit her Aunt Mary. At least Aunt Mary always appeared to be pleased to see her.

She was tired when she arrived, and her aunt was out. Linda found the key under the mat, and let herself in. The cat pretended it didn't remember her and walked off, offended, and no one (Linda thought ruefully) could look more offended than a pampered domestic cat who has been stroked by someone it has decided it doesn't know!

The little house seemed to have shrunk. Linda put down her suitcase and wandered through it, saddened because she was no longer the girl who had enjoyed staying in these small overcrowded rooms, with their chenille cloth covered tables and hand-made rugs, the litter of magazines, framed snapshots, imitation cut glass bowls of flowers from the back garden, the hand-knitted bedspreads upstairs and the hotchpotch of coverings on upholstery downstairs. Even the medley of odd china staring from the glass fronts of the cupboards was no longer the friendly thing it had been. All this that she had once loved, now stared with unfriendly eyes at her, reminding her she no longer belonged here, but was someone conditioned to satin upholstery and lush carpets, hotel life in the South of France, and a constant attendance of servants and camera-men.

She was no longer Linda, Mrs Goodge's swimming-mad niece, but a big name in Olympics, a swimming star!

The thought chilled her so much that she decided to go out. She remembered the Giant's Teeth, and getting out her swim-things, she swiftly changed into them under sweater and trews, locked up, found the old bike in the shed and cycled through Shen-stone Bay, to the rocks beyond.

All she wanted was breathing-space, time to think, to get acclimatised to being back in England. But it wasn't easy. Max had pushed everyone and everything out of her life, and dominated it all. Her love for him was like the old song said: *Deep as the ocean, high as the sky.* It wasn't possible to push him out now and to start all over again.

And this wasn't the right place to come to, for this was where she had first met Andy Blane. She could almost see him standing up there now, staring down at her. She knew now, looking back, that he had merely been assessing her value, and the chances of exploiting it. How young and unsophisticated she had been then!

The thunder rolled, and a brief flash of lightning warned her that the weather wasn't improving. She shivered. This was no way to go on, sitting here remembering things best forgotten. Much better to swim. Swimming always relaxed her, mentally and physically, and prevented her from thinking of other things.

She got up impatiently to tear off her top things. The rocks were still wet from recent rain and her foot slipped. She skidded down, on her back. There was a brief pain, then she managed to arrest her slithering by jamming her heel in a crack between two rocks.

What had she done? She moved carefully, but there appeared to be no bones broken. The best thing was to swim, vigorously, then out, rub down, cycle back to Aunt Mary's and make some good hot tea! She should have done that at first!

She dived in, not quite so neatly as usual. Perhaps she shouldn't have gone in the water so soon after slipping? Oh, what a lot of rot, she told herself angrily! Fussing over slithering down the rocks, a thing she had often done in the past and thought nothing of it! You've been pampered, my girl, she told herself crossly, and bent up double to do a little somersault in the water.

A pain like a red-hot needle shot through her back, and she fluffed it. She, who had been likened to a fish for those natural movements in the water, couldn't even somersault now! With a painfully beating heart she crawled out and sat shivering on the rocks.

Max didn't see that photograph on the front of the newspaper when he returned to France from England; he saw it after Linda had gone. He was furious. He had come back alone, determined to make up time on the film, anxious over Linda's performance and her moods, worried and astonished when he heard conflicting stories of what she had been up to. Bitterly upset that he had quarrelled with her. Frustrated when everyone had something to say against her and could apparently prove it.

'I'm going to get to the bottom of this!' he thundered. 'Blane should have known better than to allow her to make that short! Where is he? Find him for me!' No one could.

I'll have it out with Caroline, then, he decided. Caroline must deny the rumour of their re-engagement, and publicly too. Her father was better again, and anyway, he wasn't going to have his life messed up just because Joe's heart wasn't all it might be. Joe had been ill for years and would probably go on like this; down one minute, up the next. There had been no need for Caroline to go to pieces like that and now Max had the sneaking conviction that it had been for the benefit of the Press cameras! Hating himself for the thought, he sat in his chauffeur-driven car, going towards the hotel where Caroline was staying, and found himself wondering why she had come back to the Riviera, instead of staying with her father if she was so upset about him. What had she said, as the reason for her coming back? Oh, yes, there were one or two things she had to clear up!

He closed his eyes. He had, in effect, promised Joe in England that he would stay by Caroline's side. At the time, Max had taken it to be the act of a friend that was required of him; help Caroline, keep her company, during her father's illness, and until her father was up and about again. Now he wasn't so sure. Could it have been that Joe, too, had been pressing him to become engaged again to Caroline?

He was aghast. How could he have been

such a fool as to promise, without making sure? But then, how could one press a sick man to dot the i's and cross the t's? Did one ever? The thing to do was to promise the earth, to help the patient recover! But if Joe Chadwick was going to continue to have these heart attacks, where would Max be?

He felt caught. No, it couldn't have been planned – neither he nor Joe nor Caroline would do such a thing, he comforted himself! But Caroline had played that trick on the Ross family, hadn't she? No, no, she couldn't have done *this!*

He felt desperately tired. His heart ached for Linda, but because of the disparity of their ages, he had always wondered whether he would be able to keep her love, while Blane was about. Blane was the sort of young fellow who could charm a bird off a tree, and although he and Linda were always scrapping, Max didn't allow himself to think that might mean anything. She had minded so much about Blane being allowed to continue handling her smaller affairs, and to Max that meant that if Andy couldn't handle the whole of her life she didn't want to see him humiliated by the small stuff. Now she had gone, walked out of his life. She couldn't really have cared for him, to do that!

Just the same, he had got to sift the matter to the bottom with Blane, find out the whole truth of this advertisement film. He must know if Linda knew what she was doing! Meantime, there was Caroline to settle.

The reception desk knew him. 'Don't announce me,' he said. 'I'll just go up!'

The clerk nodded and smiled. If the gentleman wanted to give the lady a nice surprise, that was no affair of his. Mr Welman tipped well.

The clerk who had just gone off duty, came back in a hurry. 'Did I see Max Welman going up? You shouldn't have let him – there's another chap up there already!' But by then it was too late to stop Max – the lift was already at the top.

He went along to Caroline's apartment and was about to tap on the door, when he heard Andy Blane's voice raised above Caroline's. 'What's biting you, sweetie? I only want a bit on the side, to tide me over! I don't want the whole sum you promised – that can come later!'

'I never promised you a bean!' Caroline stormed. 'And don't call me sweetie!'

'It's a mere figure of speech,' Andy said, in a quiet voice. 'Don't think anything about it. Let's just concentrate on our little pact. Your old man was to go and talk at her to make her think you and Max were still together, right? I was to fix it that she got our friend Max in a nice old mess with the rival firm, and legal trouble pending, right? I did that, not just competently, but with artistry. Right? I saw to it that she was seen talking to chaps from the studio – oh, they just went up to her at odd times and said something idiotic, but other people *saw* them together, and are prepared to say so. And lots of people are prepared to say that they've seen Linda and me together, and are quite prepared to swear that she's still hankering for me, her old chum, even though she's making a play for your Max's money.'

'Well? So what?' Caroline said icily. 'I didn't ask for all that. I just wanted the one thing done: the ad film. You didn't have to spread yourself. That would have been enough. What my father did was none of your business.'

'Just the same, pet, you did intimate that I was to be well and truly compensated. Well, I've come for the first instalment. That's all.'

'I can't help it if you got that impression. I didn't make any promises about money, and I think you're going to be a nuisance, Andy Blane.'

'No, not if you agree to a little proposition I have. Let's settle on five thousand, in instalments – what's it to you? You'll have Welman and he's worth a fortune! – and I'll take the girl out of your hair for all time, by marrying her. What about that?'

'Chance would be a fine thing! I can't see her agreeing to that!' Caroline sneered. 'Besides, I haven't got that much money.'

'Like I said, you *will* have, when you marry Welman! As to Linda, I'll have her eating out of my hand, after I've told her a few (highly colourful and purely imaginary) things that Welman has said to lots of people about her!'

Max could stand no more. Softly he turned the handle and walked in, just as Caroline, fumbling with her purse, was saying, 'I told you, I haven't got that much money now, but here's a hundred to be going on with. *If* you marry that girl and I– *Max!*' she broke off, on a strangled note, as she looked across at the movement at the door, and saw him standing there, stiff and white with anger.

Max didn't wait to telephone Linda's uncle at the Public Baths. He hired a plane and flew to England that night.

It was three days since Linda had left him

and after the ugly scene with Caroline and Andy, there had been other things to tidy up, before he got the complete picture. Once he had it, his one thought was to get to Linda's side and to straighten everything out with her.

The family had gone to bed when the taxi went along Linda's little street, and Max leapt out almost before it had stopped. Linda's uncle was just putting out the milk bottles before bolting the front door, when Max strode up the path.

'You? At this time of night?' Zacchary said slowly. 'I confess I expected to see you earlier, but when it got so late, it seemed you weren't coming.'

'I'm sorry it's so late. I've only just flown in from France. I'd hoped to see you, my dear fellow! Can I talk to you? I take it Linda's here?'

'She is,' Zacchary said, 'but don't count on her ever wanting to see you. You see, something's happened.'

He led the way into the sitting-room, and put on the electric fire again. 'She had a bit of an accident.'

'Oh, my heavens! When? How?' Max exploded.

'I think we could both do with a nip of

this,' Zacchary said, getting his own bottle out of the sideboard, and two glasses. 'Been a bit of an upset all round, but you won't want to hear about what her mother said or did. She collapsed of course. Poor Margaret, I think sometimes it's an escape valve with her. She's always better afterwards, but we suffer for weeks.'

'Yes, but Linda!' Max pressed.

'Seems she couldn't face home, when she flew back from France. She's told me a good bit about it. Poor kid! She went to Shenstone Bay. Her aunt was out, so she went to that pool among the rocks, to have a bit of a swim and a think. She fell.'

'Oh, my heavens! Was she hurt badly?' Max choked.

'Depends on the way you look at it,' Zacchary said slowly. 'With a bit of rest, she'll be about again soon.'

'But her swimming!'

'Ah, there you have it!' Zacchary tried to light his pipe but dropped the tobacco tin, and frustrated, gave it up. 'Swimming's a funny thing. You know that.'

'For heaven's sake, speak out, man! Won't she ever swim again? Is that what you're trying to say?'

'Oh, I daresay – messing about in the water

for her own pleasure. Top-line swimming, I'm afraid, is out.'

'No! I don't believe it! I'll have a specialist—'

'I've had one,' Zacchary said quietly. 'I've a bit put by. I'm not the one to stand by and not let my niece have the best if I can afford it. It's his opinion I've given you.'

Max sat with his head in his hands. His world had crashed around his ears, and he didn't understand how or why. He had tried to do the best for everyone and had failed them all. He was lost. He didn't notice Zacchary go quietly out, muttering about making them both some coffee. He didn't hear the door quietly open when Linda came down to find out whose voice she could hear, that sounded so much like Max's voice. It was when her back hurt her suddenly and she stumbled, that he realised he wasn't alone, and looked up and saw her.

'*Linda!*' He was across the room in two strides and gathered her up in his arms. 'You shouldn't have come out of bed, you shouldn't have come down!' he said, hardly knowing what he was saying or doing.

He put her gently down on the settee. Her hair was tousled, she had no make-up on; only the old dressing-gown she had left at

235

home when she had first gone to France.

In some queer way, she had shed the veneer of sophistication, and for the first time, she looked very much like the girl he had first seen on television.

He gathered her face in his hands, unaware that his own was wet. 'There's no one but you in all the world for me,' he murmured thickly. 'How can I ever make you see that?'

'Not – Caroline?' she managed, her own voice unsteady.

'It's never been Caroline,' he told her firmly. 'I owed so much to Joe Chadwick and he wanted us to be married so badly. I let him think it was so, from heart attack to heart attack. But there's a limit to how far a man can go, and ruin his own life at the same time. I think I've done all I can for Joe Chadwick.' He searched her face. 'And now it may be too late. What have I done to you, Linda? What have I done?'

'You've given me all I ever wanted, Max,' she said shakily. 'I'm a lucky girl. What does it matter if I can't do any more international swimming? I've got to the top! I've had the best. If I can have your love, I don't want anything else.'

Zacchary came in with a tray of coffee, and saw them, locked in a close embrace, oblivious to everyone and everything. He backed out hastily, and went back to the kitchen, where he stood thinking.

So that was the way it was! Well, he hadn't much fault to find with that. He had always liked Max Welman, since he had met him in the flesh. Linda loved Max, and Max? Well, there were plenty of explanations to be done, on both sides, and things straightened out. Time for all that later. For the moment, Linda was in the arms of the man she loved, and if ever there had been devotion and anguish in a man's eyes, Zacchary had seen it in Max Welman's, when he had heard of Linda's accident.

Yes, Max loved Linda all right, and he'd no doubt manage to convince Linda of it this time, if the scene in the sitting-room just now was any indication, Zacchary thought with satisfaction, as he poured himself a cup of coffee and sat down to enjoy it.